Miss Weston's Wager

Brides of Brighton Book 4

ASHTYN NEWBOLD

Copyright © 2019 by Ashtyn Newbold
All rights reserved.

No part of this book may be reproduced in any form whatsoever, whether by graphic, visual, electronic, film, microfilm, tape recording, or any other means, without prior written permission of the publisher, except in the case of brief passages embodied in critical reviews and articles.

This is a work of fiction. The characters, names, incidents, places and dialogue are products of the author's imaginations and are not to be construed as real. Any resemblance of characters to any person, living or dead, is purely coincidental.

ISBN 13: 9781075445705

Editing by Tori MacArthur

For the imaginative and brave

Chapter 1

BRIGHTON, ENGLAND, AUTUMN 1814

Of all the things Harriett Weston enjoyed, sketching lilacs proved the most difficult. The petals, much smaller than that of the average flower, possessed intricate lines and varying shades of violet. Not only were the petals small, but there was also an abundance of them, surrounding the stem in quantities she could scarcely comprehend.

Making the endeavor of sketching them even more difficult, was the sad fact that there were no lilacs to be found on the Weston property, not now that autumn had come. The lilac was also Harriett's favorite flower. The color reminded her of joy and love, of riches and serenity. She scrunched her brow as she positioned her pencil over her sketchbook, closing her eyes as she struggled to recall the image of a lilac in her mind. She stared at the bare bush with intensity, willing a beautiful flower with pale violet petals to appear. She regretted not finishing her drawing during the summer months when the bushes had been in full bloom.

She regretted many things of late.

She dropped her pencil with frustration when her hand failed her, shaking too much to create the perfect line. Drawing usually calmed her, but Harriett found that nothing could calm her in recent months. Not with the impending return of Mr. William Harrison to Brighton.

Never had a man inflicted such ill-ease upon her like William did. It was not that he was an unpleasant man. In fact, no one seemed to be able to find a single fault in him, especially Harriett's sister, Grace. And that was where the problem had begun.

Just months before, Grace had been prattling on about her nonsensical belief that she was an expert in love, with no real experience to support such a statement. She had suggested for the hundredth time, it seemed, that Harriett court their childhood friend, Mr. William Harrison.

After much discussion, a wager had been struck between sisters, one that Harriett had quickly lost. If Grace could prove her expertise by gaining a proposal from the man of Harriett's choosing, then Harriett would agree to encourage William to court her. Harriett had deemed her own victory a sure thing, but she had been sadly mistaken.

Grace did indeed gain a proposal, and a marriage too. And now Harriett was forced to fulfill her end of the bargain. The moment William returned to Brighton, she was required to encourage him into a courtship. If he did indeed pursue a courtship with her, she was required to endure three meetings with him before she could decline his attention. The very idea set her palms sweating and her heart racing like a spooked horse.

Since the wager had been struck, Harriett had been considering every possible way out of it. Unfortunately, her sister was one of the most stubborn women of the county, with an unwavering opinion. Grace would never rest until her sister became Harriett Harrison, a name which Harriett shuddered at the thought of. Society, of course, would know her as simply Mrs. William Harrison. She cringed. Could there ever be a more boring name than that? Her friend, Rose Daventry, was soon to become Lady Gouldsmith, wed to Sir Martin Gouldsmith. Harriett longed for the excitement of such a lovely name.

It seemed her life was destined to be like the dying lilacs on the bush before her, uninteresting, dull, and mediocre.

Of course, she would never become Mrs. William Harrison. What Grace did not understand was that years ago, Harriett had given William every reason to avoid her forever. He would likely despise her now.

Although Harriett missed her sister, she was quite glad that Grace was away with her husband visiting his cousins in the north of England, far enough away that she could not scold Harriett for putting off the wager. Harriett could avoid William a little longer.

As she mused over these things, she set her pencil to her paper once more, the tip nearly breaking under the weight of her distress. At least William was not set to arrive for two weeks. Two weeks in which Harriett could enjoy her freedom. The man never failed to bring a stirring to her stomach, a mix of emotions she didn't dare puzzle out. They attended the same social events when propriety required it, and she knew he tried just as hard as she did to avoid meeting eyes, being seated near one another, or, heaven forbid, engaging in a conversation. She had spent years trying to forget her childhood memories that involved him.

And there were many.

After several minutes, Harriett outlined the final details of the largest lilac on her page, closing her sketchbook with a snap. She examined the position of the sun, judging the time to be approximately nine. She missed the mornings she had spent with Grace, sketching while her sister read books beneath trees on their property. But Grace was now married, receiving the lovely name of Lady Coventry, leaving Harriett to enjoy the company of the other unattached females of Brighton.

But Harriett's favorite female companion, Rose Daventry, was soon to abandon her as well to the marriage noose. They could still enjoy their morning walks together, but Rose would have the responsibility of running a household, leaving little time for her unmarried friends.

With a sigh, Harriett stood from her place on the garden bench, smoothing her skirts as she walked to the back door of Weston Manor. After she had replaced her sketchbook atop her writing desk and tied her favorite straw bonnet, she stepped outside to find Rose awaiting her.

Endowed with a tall and willowy figure, golden curls, and a glowing complexion, it was no surprise that Rose had made such a lovely match with Sir Martin.

Harriett met her friend with a smile. "I am in great need of a walk this morning," she said, forcing her voice to be cheerful. "Exertion is the only thing I have found capable of clearing my mind."

Rose gave her a warm smile in return. "I do enjoy our morning walks. You are the only friend I have that doesn't tire of my talk of wedding preparations." She gave a trilling laugh, as if the contrary were impossible. For the sake of her friend, Harriett didn't outwardly deny the words, though she could think of a long list of topics that would be of greater interest to her than Rose's perfect marriage. But she was happy for her friend, she truly was.

As Harriett descended the front steps, she held her skirts high, buried beneath her cloak, hoping to draw attention to them. The result was as she had hoped. Rose gasped in delight, placing one hand over her full lips. "Oh, Harriett. Is this the gown you spoke of last week?"

She nodded with vigor. It was the first day she had worn the gown. After spending weeks constructing it, she had been eager to finally wear it. "I found the fabric in town and simply could not resist it. The construction was difficult, but Mama assisted me in the intricacies. I used an old dress to structure the pieces, then added the embellishments you see here." Harriett shrugged out of her cloak and pointed at the layer of chiffon on the sleeves and the overlay of lace covering most of the lavender skirts. With honey-blonde curls and pale blue eyes, Harriett had concluded that the gentle lavender color would suit her complexion quite nicely. Her mother had wholeheartedly agreed.

Rose stepped closer to examine the gown. "It is the most exquisite thing I have ever seen you wear!" she said in a voice of delight. "It flatters your figure most becomingly. Mr. Harrison will be very pleased with it, I daresay."

Harriett's elation dropped at the mention of William. "I do not wear it with the intention to please him." She had confided in Rose concerning the consequences of her wager with Grace. She hadn't guessed her friend would be so quick to agree with her sister on the perfection of the match.

"It does not matter whether you intend to please him

or not." Rose swatted a hand through the air. "He will be pleased without your permission. I have always wished you two would marry. I could scarcely imagine a better match for you than William." Rose's expression brightened. "You must keep me informed with all the details of your courtship."

Harriett sighed. "You will be sorely disappointed. All I am required is three meetings. After they have passed I am allowed to give up the endeavor."

"And break poor William's heart? You are not the sort of woman to do that."

A surge of guilt pulsed in Harriett's chest. "This courtship is not even likely to happen." She willed herself not to appear ruffled. "William and I have known one another for our entire lives. We have been at many of the same dances and dinner parties, and he has never given me attention beyond the expected polite greeting. Not a word has passed between us since our childhood, and hardly a glance. If he wished to pursue me, he would have done so by now." A sneaking sensation of ache touched her heart. She was entirely to blame for the distance that had grown between herself and William.

Rose lifted her eyes heavenward, pursing her lips. "Oh, Harriett. He has adored you since we were children. But he was also the ear to which you cast all your dreams of marrying a man of nobility. I believe his lack of pursuit signifies the goodness of his character."

Harriett scowled. "How so?"

"He knows that to marry you, he would be robbing you of your dream. And he would never do that. He cares for you far too much."

Harriett wished she hadn't asked for clarification. She remembered the days Rose spoke of—the days she had spent countless hours with Rose and Grace on the beach near the Daventry home. William, just two years her senior, had often accompanied the girls, taking part in their games of imagination as they searched the sand for hidden treasures.

"Where shall we walk today?" Harriett asked abruptly, troubled by the direction of the conversation. "It has been days since we took the path leading through the woods." After her recent thoughts, Harriett did not feel inclined to see the beach.

"The woods sound like just the thing," Rose said. "The birds are very musical at this time of day. We are sure to find a greater abundance among the trees than along the beach. And we may enjoy the changing colors of the leaves."

Harriett nodded her agreement, linking her arm through Rose's as they set off toward the woods. The morning air carried the scent of moisture and vegetation, and the sun had only recently finished its ascent above the coastline. Rose immediately began speaking of the numerous details of her wedding, details which she had already given Harriett on multiple occasions. As they entered the cover of the woods, Harriett found her thoughts traveling elsewhere, but made sure to offer the periodic, "I see," or "how wonderful," to keep her friend appeased.

She studied the broad trunks, the sturdy and mottled wood of the trees, noting her preference to the woods over the ocean. Trees were predictable and strong, unyielding to their surroundings. In contrast, the ocean turned to and fro as the wind demanded, tossing the water in unforgiving waves. Harriett had once preferred the ocean, as it inspired her childhood imagination. But as she had grown and matured, she had become rigid and unimaginative like the trees.

"Did you hear what I said?" Rose's voice broke through her thoughts as they approached a fallen tree at the start of a clearing.

Harriett looked up at her friend's partially raised brow. "I'm afraid I must have missed it."

Rose sighed, but instead of appearing disappointed in Harriett, her lips pursed in a mischievous smirk. "You were thinking of William again, weren't you?"

"I am sorry to disappoint you, but no, I was not." Harriett placed a finger between her neck and bonnet ribbons, feeling hot despite the cool air.

Prancing forward through a patch of fallen leaves, Rose spun around to face her. "Do you remember when we pretended we were pirates in search of treasure? William was the captain, you were the quartermaster, I was the cooper, and Grace was the carpenter." Rose fell into a fit of giggles. "Grace demanded that she be the quartermaster instead, but you refused to abandon the role. You two had many quarrels over that."

Harriett scolded her lips for smiling, pulling her mouth back into a firm line. "How ridiculous we all were."

Rose stopped, one eyebrow raised. "Ridiculous? It was your idea."

"And what a ridiculous idea it was." Harriett pulled her cloak tightly around herself, hoping her expression conveyed passiveness and not the memories that haunted her. "Our days would have been better spent within doors practicing our instruments, stitching, and French."

Rose gaped at her in a most unladylike fashion. "Do you not look upon those days as the most thrilling of your life? Being a child is an opportunity that never comes again. When a person is grown, they are censured for overuse of their imagination, but as a child, it is encouraged."

Harriett did not feel inclined to explain to Rose why she looked at those days with regret. She had every reason to. "It was an enjoyable time, I will confess, but I grew out of it."

"Rather abruptly," Rose mumbled. "You were there one day and gone the next. William stopped coming too."

Harriett clasped her hands in front of her. "Good. He was far too old to be playing pretend."

As they approached the fallen tree, Harriett stopped, examining the breadth of the trunk. "How could a tree of this size have fallen?" She stepped on top of it before climbing down to the other side. She extended her hand to Rose, offering to help her over. The place where the roots had once taken hold was covered in vines and leaves.

"I haven't the slightest idea." Rose grasped Harriett's hand, climbing and then alighting from the trunk with ease. She bent over to brush bits of leaves off the bottom half of her skirts, looping her arm through Harriett's as they continued on the path.

A grin tugged at Harriett's lips. "I thought you would suggest that a group of ruffians, recently escaped from Bedlam, capsized the tree in an attempt to trap us the entire day and night in a dark forest."

"That would have been my first conjecture, but you just claimed imagination to be ridiculous." Rose raised one eyebrow.

The steady and unmistakable sound of horse hooves struck the ground in the distance, calling Harriett's eyes over her shoulder.

"Who might that be?" Rose asked, her hazel eyes twinkling in curiosity. "One of these ruffians you speak of?"

Harriett stared at the fallen log, biting her lower lip. "We ought to warn the rider of the fallen tree, even if he is a ruffian." She started walking in the direction of the sound, Rose trailing close behind. She stopped several feet behind the log, crossing her arms. "Should we wait here until we catch sight of the rider?"

Rose nodded, squinting past the clearing and into the woods, where the hoofbeats grew louder. "He is riding quite quickly."

"A skilled rider and agile horse would have no problem avoiding the tree, even if it did come upon them unexpectedly." Harriett considered calling out to the distant rider, but doubted her voice would be heard. She moved to the side of the log to ensure she was out of the way if the rider intended to send his horse leaping over it.

Her heart pounded with dread. The rider was not slowing down. He would only see the log the moment he came into the clearing, and she suspected his horse would not have time to react.

"Sir!" she called out, as loud as her lungs would allow. She waved her arms in the air, and Rose joined her in the motion. "Sir!"

The warning didn't reach the rider in time. A white horse came bounding through the trees and reared back hard, throwing its rider forcefully to the ground. The man landed near the horse's feet before the creature's back leg struck him in the head with such force that he was thrown onto his back several feet away. Harriett covered her mouth with both hands. The rider lay motionless, still too close to his horse's stamping feet to be safe. Harriett rushed forward without thinking, her muscles sparking with desperation. The man could easily be trampled again.

"Harriett!" Rose's dismayed voice was mingled with a gasp.

Heart pounding, Harriett moved first toward the agitated horse, attempting to calm it. Her family owned many fine horses, and while Harriett had not taken a great deal of interest in them growing up, she had seen her father calm them on many occasions. The first step was to remain calm herself. She pressed down her fear as she approached the animal, speaking softly to it as she extended her hand to stroke its side. The horse's coat glistened with sweat, its muscled body fatigued. Eventually its breathing slowed, and it became still.

"Harriett." The terror in Rose's voice sent a wave of unease through Harriett's stomach. She glanced in the direction of her voice. Rose stood above the fallen rider, her brow drawn together in deep concern.

Was he *dead*?

Harriett swallowed hard, leaving the horse's side to assist Rose. She stopped when she saw the man's face as he lay motionless on the ground. His dark auburn hair, dark eyebrows, and solid jaw were all too familiar. Her blood froze, her skin grew cold, and her heart galloped faster than any horse. She could see only his profile, but it was enough to know with certainty the rider's identity.

It was William.

"Do you think he's alive?" Rose's voice was taut, filled with dread. "Shall I fetch my father to help?"

Harriett fell to her knees in front of him, her hands shaking as she felt for his pulse, brushed her fingers under his nose. A faint heat touched her cold hands, the rustle of air from his lungs. She sighed in relief. What the devil was William doing in Brighton? Harriett had just spoken to his sister Maria three days before. Maria had said

William would not be returning for two weeks. What had compelled him to race through the woods in such an eager manner? She searched his head with her gloved fingertips, looking for the source of the blood that spilled into the dirt and leaves beneath him. Her own head was becoming faint, her stomach a tight ball.

Rose kept her distance, trembling. "I will fetch my father."

Harriett heard her retreating footfalls, heavy and fast.

She found the place William's head had been struck, her glove coming away wet with blood. The horse had kicked with enough force to split the skin. She took off her cloak, wadding the fabric and pressing it against the wound. With all her strength, she turned him over by tucking her hands around his torso. She leaned over him to press her ear to his chest. His heart beat slowly, softly, as if it were almost too weary to continue. His face was white, his breathing shallow. Panic seized in her chest.

"William," she said. "Open your eyes. Please, open your eyes."

Her words were not greeted by even a flutter of his eyelids, not even a twitch. She studied his face, pressing the cloak harder against his head as she did. She had once punctured her finger with a needle, and her father had told her to apply pressure to the wound. "Please wake up, William."

Since her last day at the beach, she had not seen him in such close proximity. She had been avoiding it for so long. But now, with no choice in the matter, she noted all the things that had changed. His freckles had faded, his skin smooth, except around his mouth and jaw, where faint, dark stubble grew. His hair was a deeper red than it had once been, almost brown. His features were no longer youthful, but firm and masculine, his cheek and brow bones prominent, his eyes deep set.

She wished he would open them. She glanced behind her, desperation clawing at her composure. Rose needed to return soon.

Turning her gaze back to William, Harriett thought of another day, a much happier one, when he had looked very much the same. Only much younger, and much less pale and bloodied.

Chapter 2

TEN YEARS BEFORE

"William! Open your eyes!" Harriett shook his shoulder, giggling between her words. "I know you are not sleeping."

Sand mingled with his hair, which appeared almost the same color of the sunset behind the ocean. His eyelids twitched. So did the corners of his mouth.

"I saw that!" she said, her eyes narrowing down at his face. She poked his cheek, sitting back on her heels. "If you are truly sleeping, then you will not care if I pour water on your face, will you?"

She stood up, taking tentative steps toward the sea, the water lapping over the sand. She stepped in, just far enough to reach her ankles. Cupping her hands, she scooped up the salty water, hurrying back to William's side as it leaked through her fingers. "I will give you to the count of three to open your eyes, or I will drop this water on your face." Harriett tried to keep her voice stern, but she could not help but smile. "One, Two—"

William's mouth had slipped into a wide grin, his eyes still closed. His body shook with laughter.

"Three." Harriett opened her hands, letting the water fall over his grinning face.

He sputtered into laughter, sitting up and wiping the water from his hair and eyes. "Thank you," he said, his voice strained as he blinked rapidly against the salty water. "That was quite refreshing."

Harriett turned around, exchanging an exasperated look with Grace and Rose, who stood watching with giggles of their own. William's green eyes danced with amusement.

"We did not finish our game," Harriett said, brushing sand from her skirts as she stood. She did not care to hear another of his explanations about how he loved the sea, and the water, and being splashed in the face, and how it was nothing of a true punishment, although she knew his mama would never let him get in the sea. He knew as little about swimming as Harriett did. "You mustn't fall asleep until we are finished." She pulled him to his feet. "You cannot keep your place as captain of our ship if you insist on sleeping. Who will steer us to safety?"

"You are the quartermaster. The duty would fall to you." William's dripping hair fell over his brow, a smirk twisting his lips.

Harriett considered his words, tapping her chin. She, the captain? "Very well. Then you may go back to sleep." She hurried over to her sister and Rose, raising her hand in the air. "I sense a storm coming! Back to your positions!" Gripping the imaginary wheel, she turned the ship away from the fearsome oncoming waves.

"Unacceptable!" William stepped forward. "I am the captain, and I am feeling quite refreshed from the water that my quartermaster so willingly deposited on my head. I will take the ship from here."

"You abandoned your crew!" Harriett raised her chin. "Their loyalty belongs to me now."

Rose shook her head, speaking in a whisper, as if a louder voice would disrupt the charade they were performing. "No, I am still quite loyal to Captain William. He is much better at playing captain."

Harriett gasped when her sister nodded in agreement.

"We vote to allow Captain William a pardon, just this once," Grace exclaimed, raising her own fist in the air.

Harriett stepped grudgingly aside, allowing William to take the invisible wheel. He grinned in triumph, but his smile softened when he saw Harriett's disappointment. "You may be captain if you really wish to be, Harriett." His voice was a whisper in her ear, low enough to evade Rose and Grace's attention. "I could pretend to be injured."

Her anger faded the moment he used that voice on her—the sweet, considerate, and kind one. Her anger always mounted at his mischievous smirks and triumphant voices, but he could quickly put out the flame within seconds. "No. The crew has spoken." She stepped away from him, coming to a stop beside her sister.

He quirked an eyebrow in her direction, curiosity in his gaze. He seemed to still be examining her, searching for any sign of her unrest. Harriett knew he was never content when she wasn't. "Well," he said, "this is my ship, so I do not require a pardon from you scurvy rascals." Half his mouth lifted in a smile as he pretended to whip the wheel toward the oncoming waves. "Together we with weather the storm!"

"Huzzah!" The three girls shouted. Harriett laughed at the mad motions William made as he pretended to steer the ship away from danger. She pretended to be tossed to and fro along the planks of their ship, her half boots filling with sand and smooth pebbles.

"Do you see that?" William pointed ahead at the ocean. With her eyes, Harriett saw nothing but a calm sea and fading horizon, but her imagination saw much more. She imagined the writhing tentacles of a sea creature, rising above the waves and wriggling toward their ship, the suckers moving to pull them into the depths of the stormy sea.

"Has Arabella returned again?" Harriett ran up beside him, pretending to look through a telescope.

"Indeed, she has. The monster has not finished with us. Prepare for battle!"

Harriett grinned, exchanging a look of excitement with William. Part of her wondered if William truly enjoyed playing pretend as much as she did, or if he only did it to please her. She wasn't certain which answer she preferred. He was thirteen. Most thirteen year old boys of Brighton were away at school, or spent their time learning to hunt or shoot or studying at the side of a tutor. But when William was not kept to his house, he always preferred to play with Harriett, Grace, and Rose.

Harriett pretended to prepare her cannon, and William commanded that they hold their fire. He steered their imaginary ship closer to Arabella, the name they had chosen for the sea creature. William shouted for them to fire the cannons, and all three girls obeyed, giggling.

"Oh, blast it!" Harriett said. "The creature has escaped!"

William smiled at her. "I suppose we must fight it again tomorrow."

She took a steadying breath, in part because of the thrill of the recent battle, and in part because of the fluttering William's smile planted in her stomach. She would never admit to Grace and Rose that she liked William so much. She usually just complained to them about his teasing, pretending she didn't like it as much as she did.

"Do you suppose she is immortal?" William asked, shielding his eyes from the sun as he gazed at the ocean. "No matter how many cannons we fire at her she will not be defeated."

Harriett grinned. She liked the idea of having an immortal monster to defeat. "I suppose she is immortal."

"So we shall have to fight her forever."

Harriett raised her chin. "We shall never give up."

Harriett imagined that William was not really so injured, and that his head had stopped bleeding. She imagined that he opened his warm green eyes and smiled at her.

Her fingers flitted over his hair, brushing it away from his forehead. She strained to turn her head over her shoulder, searching for any sign of Rose in the trees. What could she do? Fear pounded through her veins with a new energy she had never felt before.

Waiting was excruciating, especially when one didn't know what they were waiting for. Was she waiting for him to open his eyes? To take a deep breath? To take his last? She hushed her last thought, the stabbing in her heart shocking her. William had been her dearest friend. Regret—deep, stinging regret—struck her then, sudden and intense.

At last, after several agonizing minutes, Rose's father crashed through the woods with a pair of servants, and the town physician, Mr. Gibbs, close behind. He dismounted from his horse and rushed to William's side. Harriett stood, making room for him to do his work.

"Will he be all right?" she asked.

Mr. Gibbs didn't say a word as he prodded William, testing his pulse, the wound on his head, and the temperature of his forehead. His brow was tight when he straightened, beckoning Rose's father and the two servants closer. "We must move him some place more comfortable. The bleeding has slowed, but there will be an immediate need for stitches. His neck appears to be unharmed, but the blow to his head is quite severe."

Harriett's stomach turned over and over, flipping like a fish on the sand. She watched the men transfer William to the cart they had brought, tied behind one of the horses. The surgeon wrapped William's head in a thick bandage. "Where is this man's residence?"

"Only a half mile east of mine, sir," Rose's father, Mr. Daventry, responded. "I will accompany you." He turned to his daughter. "Finish your walk with Miss Weston as planned. You would do well to forget the horrific scene you have witnessed." Her father gave her a sympathetic look before mounting his horse and following the surgeon and William out of the clearing.

Rose turned toward Harriett, her cheeks flushed from her recent exertion. "I do hope he will be all right." She clutched Harriett's hand. "Oh, poor William."

Harriett's thoughts raced and roared in her mind, and she did not have the strength to contend with them. "He has always been quite strong. I believe he will recover." Her voice shook. Until that moment, seeing William helpless and broken, Harriett had not dared examine her feelings toward him. Well—at least she had not dared allow herself to dwell on them for longer than a few seconds.

"Why do you suppose he returned to Brighton two

weeks early?" Rose asked. "He seemed to be attending to a very urgent matter.".

"I do not know." Harriett stared at the place where William had fallen. As a child, William had seemed as though nothing could hurt him. He had always shown confidence and strength. The image of him today would haunt her forever.

"Shall we pay him a visit tomorrow, to ensure he is well?"

Harriett did not know what would frighten her more—seeing William still unconscious or finding him awake. Then she would be forced to encourage a courtship with him as a result of her blasted wager.

Grace would not be returning to Brighton for at least two months, she reminded herself. Harriett could put off her wager until then. For now, her only concern was William's recovery.

The onslaught of emotions within her were too much. She needed to be alone to sort through them. "I suppose paying William a visit would be a polite thing to do." Her head pounded as her anxiety continued to surge.

"That was quite brave of you, saving his life like that," Rose said.

Harriett frowned. "I did not save his life."

"I told the physician everything. You calmed the horse to ensure it did not kick him again."

Oh, yes. She had nearly forgotten amid the whirlwind she had just experienced. Her head pounded and ached.

They cut their walk short, circling back to Rose's home rather than taking the long route through the woods. After Rose left, Harriett finished the walk home alone, her feet skimming the ground as she sped over the path and back lawn of her house. Her limbs still shook with the events of the past hour, and worry enveloped her senses. What would happen to William? She couldn't bear the thought of him suffering, even if she didn't particularly wish to court him, as her sister desired. So many memories flooded her thoughts, a pool so deep she couldn't even begin to swim through it.

As she walked into the house, one of their maids, Rebecca, took her bonnet. "Good mornin,' Miss Harriett. How was your walk? Why didn't you take a cloak? 'Tis quite a bone-chillin day."

Harriett didn't have the energy to explain what had transpired, at least not to Rebecca. Besides, she knew Rebecca to be a gossip of the most incorrigible sort. Surely William would not wish his current condition known by all the servants in Brighton. "It was very diverting," she said, attempting to evoke a light tone. Her body still trembled and her pulse raced. She hoped it would escape Rebecca's notice.

Rebecca gave a warm smile. "I'm glad to hear that. And you'll be glad to hear that your Uncle, the Baron of Hove's in the drawing room with a surprise for you. Lookin' the likes of a shining candle, so bright and excited-like he was." Rebecca's eyes shifted downward, settling on Harriett's hands. "Miss!" She gasped. "What happened?"

Harriett followed the maid's gaze. The fingers of her right glove were stained with William's blood. Her stomach lurched and twisted.

"You is lookin' quite pale, miss." Rebecca's concerned voice flitted through Harriett's spinning mind, the lightness in her head sharp and insistent. She blinked down at her bloodied hand one more time before darkness flooded up and up, until it swallowed her completely.

Chapter 3

Harriett had never fainted before. She had never had a reason to. She was not nearly as weak-stomached as most young ladies, and she had claimed that quality with pride. But William's blood upon her fingers had been enough to send her collapsing to the ground like a horse might have on four broken legs, or so Rebecca had told her when she finally opened her eyes.

Searing pain throbbed in her right temple, where her head had struck the solid floor. Mid morning light came through the nearby windows of the drawing room, warming her skin and adding to the perspiration on her forehead. She lifted her hand in front of her face, relieved to see that the blood had been washed from it, and the glove had been taken away to be washed or disposed of.

The crystal blue eyes of her Uncle Cornelius, the respectable Baron of Hove, blinked at her from above.

"Good heavens, you look dreadful, my dear. I hope your sudden fainting had nothing to do with my news."

Harriett groaned as she sat up, her head throbbing. Curiosity cut through the pain enough for her to inquire after his meaning. "News? I have not received any news."

His expression tightened into a serious one, a look she wasn't accustomed to seeing on her uncle's usually jovial face. "I fear I cannot tell you now. I should hate to be the cause of your fainting a second time."

What could he mean? Her curiosity only grew. Before she could ask again, her mother appeared beside Uncle Cornelius, her brow knit with concern. "I have instructed Rebecca to fetch a cold rag for your head. I have also sent for the physician." Her mother waved a collection of smelling salts under Harriett's nose, awakening her senses abruptly in a rush of rosemary and mint.

"Mama, you needn't fetch the physician. He is quite busy with much more important matters today." Harriett flinched as she touched the side of her head, which had already begun swelling into a lump. "What is the news, uncle?" Harriett doubted she would faint again. Nothing could be more shocking than what she had already seen and endured that morning.

"No, no, Cornelius. Do not say a word." Her mother's worry was evident in her voice, clipped and frantic. She turned back to Harriett. "You must answer my questions first. How do you know that the physician is busy? And why was your hand covered in blood, when I have found no injuries on you?"

Harriett wasn't fond of the idea of reliving the events of that day in her mind, but it seemed her mother would insist on it. "I took a walk with Rose this morning, as you know, and—"

Her mother gasped. "Was Rose hurt?"

"No—a gentleman was hurt."

"Who?"

Harriett sighed. As she relayed the event, her mother's eyes seemed to double in size, round and filled with shock. "Oh, my dear, girl. A young lady should never be forced to endure such horrific things." She pulled Harriett into her arms. "If only you had married already, then you would not have been on that walk with Rose, and you would not have found yourself in such a situation."

Her mother's warm embrace did nothing to lessen the sting of her words. Harriett knew how disappointed her mother was that she was still unmarried. Within a year or two, the word spinster might as well be branded across Harriett's forehead. It didn't help her case that her sister, two years her junior, had married first. And an earl, no less.

"How foolish of Mr. Harrison to ride so carelessly," her mother said. "If not for the fallen tree, the horse could have trampled you instead. Thank goodness the tree interfered with his reckless riding." She huffed a breath, stroking her hand over Harriett's hair.

"Mama! You cannot be glad he was so injured."

She sighed. "I am not glad he was injured, but I am glad he didn't bring you harm. I do not like him. He is far too quiet and reserved and gives himself an air of pridefulness. To hear that he is injured is of no consequence to me."

Uncle Cornelius made a sound of swift disapproval. "I know Mr. Harrison quite well, and I find him most amiable. I will pay him a visit later. Harriett, would you like to accompany me?"

"Good heavens, Cornelius! She was just injured herself, as a result of her being in the presence of that man's carelessness. I will not have her visiting him as if she owes him any kind of service. She practically saved his life already."

Her uncle's eyes were still turned in Harriett's direction, ignoring his sister's interjection. "It might cheer you up?" There was a gleam of mischief in his gaze, the suggestion that he was as much in favor of her courting William as Grace was.

But Harriett did not want to dwell on William any longer. It was doing dangerous things to her heart and composure. She did not want to think of him lying there so helpless and hurt. She put on a weak smile. "If you wish to bring me cheer, you will stop teasing me and tell me the news you came here to deliver."

Uncle Cornelius chuckled, straightening his posture and his jacket in one motion. He wore his favorite bright yellow waistcoat, the buttons stretched over his round belly. Before speaking, he fetched his cane, which rested against a nearby chair. "Very well." He turned to his sister, exchanging a bright smile with her. Harriett breathed a sigh of relief. At least the news couldn't be dreadful if it earned such a smile from her disconcerted mother. Uncle Cornelius chuckled. "You would be wise to keep the smelling salts near." He winked at Harriett before giving his cane a swing in front of him.

His expression turned exuberant and playful. "Just the other day, I was pondering over a certain sum of money in my possession, which I have nothing to do with. I have all the property I desire, all the clothing and accessories, though I have held in reserve enough to keep my shopping habits satisfied for what remains of my days." He shared a meaningful look with Harriett. She well understood the need to keep such funds untouched. Shopping was one of her absolute favorite pastimes. She could spend hours at the Brighton shops, even if she didn't have the money to purchase a single thing.

"And so," he continued, "as I was pondering over these funds, I was stricken with an idea, though I feared your mother and father would not accept it. However, after much begging on my part, they have accepted my generosity toward you."

Harriett's heart thudded with anticipation.

"You are a handsome young lady, Harriett, and I have been saddened to see you without a season in London. I daresay you would be the most desirable woman in every ballroom."

Harriett tried to process his words, her thoughts spinning. Was he implying that he planned to send her to London? As outlandish as the idea seemed, she could not deny it. Yes, it seemed he was.

"We have been planning this surprise since Grace's marriage. I wish for nothing more than to see you so comfortably and happily settled. I have made all the arrangements to send you to London with your mother come January. I have worked out the expenses of the trip to include a new wardrobe of gowns with any embellishments you desire, as well as slippers, boots, bonnets, jewelry, headpieces, and other necessary finery."

Harriett gaped at him, her head swimming. Her uncle had been right to warn her over the prospect of fainting. *A season?* It seemed all of her dreams were coming true, all within a matter of seconds.

"Uncle Cornelius," she half whispered. "You mustn't be so generous! I—I cannot possibly take so much."

"My mind is made up, my dear. As you well know, nothing can change my mind once it is made up." His smile was wide and genuine. He seemed to find more happiness in giving his money away than having it in the first place. "I will be honored to see you make a wonderful match in London. All I wish for you is to be happy."

How could Harriett be anything but happy after receiving such news? Elation built inside her until she could hardly breathe, and tears of gratitude stung behind her eyes. How could a day that began so terribly take such a fortuitous turn? If William had not fallen from his horse that morning, Harriett could have easily declared this to be the best day of her life. "Thank you," she choked out, her cheeks aching from the breadth of her smile. "You are the most generous and kind uncle in the entire world."

Her uncle's eyes pooled at the words, and he withdrew a lace handkerchief to dab at his tears. She had never known a softer heart than his.

"I hope I have not intensified your headache with this news."

She laughed. "It is only dreadful news that causes a headache. Agreeable news will do nothing but alleviate it, I am sure."

Her mother, who had been silently listening with great rapture, clutched her hand. "We have less than three months to prepare. We must ensure your etiquette, manners, and conversation are all in alignment with what will be expected of you. Your governess was rather inept, so I will take on the responsibility of teaching you. We will choose designs only from the most recent fashion plates. There is no room for error. When you enter London, I am confident you will be an object of fascination. You are quite beautiful, but you are also several years older than most debutants. Society will wonder why we have been hiding you. We must show them there is no fault to be found in your character or appearance."

Harriett nodded, the excitement within her suddenly too much to be contained by a tiny drawing room and a stiff sofa. "I am feeling much better now, Mama. We might go to town now to begin making arrangements."

Uncle Cornelius laughed the same moment her mother did. "Let us not forget you have been through quite the ordeal this morning," she said. "You must rest."

Harriett's concern for William came flooding back, dampening her elevated mood. How could she rest when she knew he was in such dire straits? How could she rest when she knew she would be in attendance at London's upcoming season? The combination of worry and excitement wouldn't allow her a moment of sleep. There was nothing that hindered sleep more than an overactive mind.

To appease her mother and uncle, she nodded. After thanking her uncle again, her mother and Rebecca guided her up the staircase, one woman on each of her elbows, as if she were as fragile as a glass saucer.

After laying in her bed and closing her eyes, her mother and maid finally took their leave. The moment the door clicked behind them, Harriett slid out of her blankets and sat at her writing desk. Her room was filled with ribbons and fabrics, draped over furnishings and propped against the walls. She loved creating gowns and accessories almost as much as she enjoyed buying them.

Preparing a fresh sheet of foolscap, she tapped the plume of her quill against her lips. The many thoughts racing through her brain were likely the cause of the pressure and pain in her head. She needed a way to release them. Dipping the quill in the inkwell, she let it hover over the paper before she wrote:

Necessary steps to take in preparation for London:

1. Improve my knowledge of fashion and assist in the creation of the most beautiful gowns I have ever worn, and create hems of such intricacy and embellishment that they put to shame all other hems that have ever brushed the floor of Almack's.

2. Decorate my own bonnets, so that when I am asked where the handsome accessory was made, I may claim it as a work of my own hand, thus adding to my accomplishments in the eye of all potential suitors.

3. Learn a new number on the pianoforte, one that will be begged to be performed at every social assembly.

Harriett picked up her quill, studying the list. There was much more she could write, but decided to focus on just three for now, rather than overwhelm herself. This season was her chance to prove that she was capable of making a successful match, even at her age.

Hope clutched her tightly in the chest. Her family's humble properties had been suffering in recent months, bringing in little income, and her father's debts were extensive. There was no way they could have afforded to fund a season. Grace's advantageous match had yielded connections with the upper class that could help their current status, but Harriett could not help feeling that she was still a burden. Her family's finances were not yet secure, she had seen it in the creases of worry on her mother's forehead, and the late nights her father spent in his study. She wanted to make a match just as prestigious, if not more so, than Grace's. She owed it to her parents, and to herself, and now to her uncle. It had been a long while since Harriett had seen such a smile on her mother's face as she had seen today while speaking of their travels to London.

Harriett had always dreamed of marrying well, at least since her cousin Emily came to visit, who had taught Harriett all there was to know about securing a good husband. Harriett had never given much thought to the idea of love. But now that she was older, she shunned the idea entirely. There was so much more to aspire to than Grace's silly ideas. Grace had married for love, but Harriett would not bother herself with the requirement. If she happened to fall in love with a wealthy peer, then she would be pleased. If not, then she could still be happy with the living he provided, and the elevation he provided her family in society.

Her thoughts came to an abrupt halt when she remembered her wager with Grace. She was still required to see William three times. Could she count today as the first? No, her conscience wouldn't allow it. Certainly Grace meant that they both needed to be *awake* and not on the brink of death. Based on the events of that day, it seemed fate did not wish for Harriett to court William at all. First, he fell off his horse, and could quite possibly never awaken. Second, she had learned that she would be leaving for London in a few short months. To court William now would not be fair to him.

Surely Grace wouldn't encourage the match once she learned of Harriett's season. After all the money Uncle Cornelius would be investing in her, Harriett couldn't return from London unmarried. She had to make the rest of her family proud, even if it meant disappointing her sister.

Harriett did not have time to concern herself with William. Yes, she dearly hoped he recovered, but after that, she would continue on as she had for so many years with great success—forgetting him. It hadn't been easy at first, but then it had gotten easier. Since that morning, however, she felt as if she were in those early stages of forgetting all over again, and it bothered her.

Why was the blasted man so difficult to forget?

Chapter 4

William Harrison, dazed, hurting, and utterly confused, had never felt more dreadful in his entire life.

In fact, the only reason he knew his name was indeed William Harrison, was because the physician that stood above him had told him so. Why the devil would he ever have the need to verify his own name?

The back left side of his head stung and ached, the pain spreading over his entire skull. He lifted his hand to touch it, but the physician grabbed his wrist before he could.

"The stitches will need to remain uninterrupted, or they will not heal properly." The man's gruff voice brought William to attention. Did he know this man? He felt he should have recognized him, but his mind was rather blank.

"Where am I?" William asked, his voice hoarse and low. He cleared his parched throat, studying the shabby draperies and furnishings of the small room.

"You are in the drawing room of your home, sir." The physician's thick eyebrows lowered over his steel eyes. "Do you not recognize it?"

"No, no, I do now." William recognized the antique pianoforte in the corner, and the shelf of books at his right. But it still did not feel as familiar as it ought to be. "What happened to me?" Although his mind was as muddled as a swamp, he knew enough to realize that he had taken a severe blow to his head. The pain was intense.

"You were riding at an extreme pace through the woods. Two young ladies witnessed your horse leap at a fallen tree and throw you to the ground. Your horse then spooked and kicked you in the head."

William couldn't remember any of it. His horse? What color was his horse? What was his name? Or *her* name? He rubbed his forehead. "It must have been a very hard blow."

"It was, to be sure. You are quite fortunate the ordeal was witnessed."

William nodded, his mind still racing in aimless directions. There seemed to be thousands of thoughts, memories, and images within his brain, but he could not grasp onto a single one long enough to understand it. He felt as if they were all still there, but simply playing a cruel game of hide-and-seek.

"Am I skilled at riding?"

"Apparently not." The physician's eyes gleamed with mirth. "How fascinating. You have forgotten a great deal."

"That is not fascinating at all." William groaned. "It is frustrating."

"I have never encountered a patient with head trauma that induced memory-loss before." The physician shuffled through his case, withdrawing a paper and pencil.

"Please, tell me, how much of this day are you able to recall?"

William's skin bristled with annoyance, not so much at the physician, but at his fading memory. Even now, as he lay reclined, he felt his memories slipping further and further away. "I recall nothing prior to awakening in this bed."

"Sofa," the physician corrected with a look of concern.

William looked down at the torn brocade fabric beneath him. "Yes, sofa." He shook his head gently in an effort to clear it. The motion sent a stab of pain through his skull.

"And what do you recall of yourself in regard to your age, profession, and appearance?"

"I—er—" he paused. It should not have been so difficult. He squeezed his eyes shut before opening them and examining his hands. They appeared young, strong, not aged like the physician's. "I suppose I am in my twenties."

"You suppose?"

William nodded.

"You are three and twenty."

"So I was correct."

The physician ignored his comment, scribbling away on his paper. "And your profession?"

William eyed the bookshelf next to him, where a series of thick-spined law books rested in a neat row. Without hesitation, he said, "I am a barrister." His confidence grew. Perhaps his memory would return quickly.

The physician appeared surprised and pleased. "Yes, you are. And your appearance? What colors are your hair and your eyes?"

He experienced a moment of sheer disillusion. Though he had remembered his occupation, he could not recall his own appearance. It panicked him. He felt so distant from himself that he could be sitting across the room from himself and not know it. But just as the panic set in, so did his recollection. He slumped in relief. "I have dark hair, slightly auburn, with green eyes."

"Very good." The physician stole a quick glance at William's eyes to verify his words. His eyes were green, weren't they? Now he was uncertain. "Tell me about your family."

William paused. He waited for an image of his mother, or his father, or…were there more than that? He couldn't recall if he had brothers or sisters. He couldn't emerge with any description or recollection of his parents from his mind. Did he have parents? Well, of course he had parents, but did he know them? "I—" He clamped his mouth closed, searching again. The only things that existed in his world at the moment were himself, his surroundings, and the irksome, note-jotting physician. "I haven't the slightest idea," he finished with a sigh.

The man folded his paper, apparently noticing William's distress for the first time. "Come now, all will be well eventually. Most medical journals I have studied have accounted for a recovery of lost memory within a short period of time. Depending on the severity of the injury, of course." He fiddled with the corner of his notes. "But you might like to know that I am a friend of your family's. They live on the other side of Brighton, near the pavilion, your older brother Percival, your sister Maria, and your mother and father. You, as a younger son, of course, took up a profession and rented this home not long ago. You seem to enjoy your independence, but as I understand it, you visit your family often between your circuits and cases as barrister. They have come to see you several times since your injury, but you were still quite unconscious. They will be glad to hear you are awake and well. Er—sort of well, I suppose. I'm certain they will be quite disconcerted that you do not remember them."

They had come to see him *several* times? "How long have I been unconscious?"

"Oh…" The physician hesitated, casting his eyes upward in thought. "Just short of three days."

William suddenly became aware of the stabbing pain of hunger in his stomach and the stiffness of his muscles. He needed to move, to eat, to go visit his family. With all the strength he possessed, he swung his legs off the sofa. It sent a jarring pain into the back of his head. He drew a sharp breath.

"What on earth are you doing?" The physician fixed him with a glare. "Do you suppose you can simply get up and carry on after an injury such as this?" He tossed his hands toward him, motioning for him to set his legs on the cushion again.

"No, I assure you, I am able." William moved slower, shifting his hands behind him to press himself upward. Once in a sitting position, he paused, closing his eyes until the pounding in his head subsided.

"If you fall over and strike your head again, you will be putting all the work of myself and the young lady that saved your life to waste."

"A young lady saved my life?" He opened his eyes in surprise.

"Indeed. I do believe if she had not been present to calm your horse and staunch the flow of blood from your head, you would be in much more dire straits than you are now."

William's curiosity piqued. "Then I must express my

gratitude. When I feel well enough, I must call upon her. I cannot imagine it was a pleasant scene for a lady to witness."

"Frightened out of her mind, she was. I had never seen a woman so shaking and pale. Yet she was very brave, and for that I give her credit."

Compassion and gratitude surged inside him, the first positive feelings that had passed through him since he had awoken. He made to stand, but the physician caught hold of his elbow. "Not today. You may call upon her tomorrow, once you have eaten and washed and rested. Trust me when I say that you will not wish to be seen by this young lady in your current state. She is one you will wish to impress, I assure you." The physician gave the slightest of smiles.

"What is her name?" William asked.

"Miss Harriett Weston. She is the eldest Weston daughter, and quite accomplished, I hear."

William searched the records of his mind for the woman the physician had called Harriett Weston.

As expected, he found nothing.

Chapter 5

Dearest Harriett,

The northern coast is so very different from Brighton, but it is every bit as lovely. The sky is darker here and the weather is a bit severe in the way of wind and precipitation, but the ocean makes me feel as if I have not left home. Edward's cousins are very agreeable and were quick to give me a tour of all that is to be discovered in Berwick. Edward teases me over my fascination with the dark rock of the coastline, but I am only so fascinated because of how different it is from Brighton's pale pebbles and sand. I cannot wait to see what else I will discover during our time here.

How is life in Brighton? Please write me promptly when Mr. Harrison returns, and write all the details of your interactions with him. I wished Edward's relatives hadn't chosen this month to invite us here, for I had so looked forward to seeing you begin your courtship with William. You two are the perfect match, and I will never cease to say it. Pray, do not forget our wager. It was your idea, after all. You will hate me for teasing you, but I think you could have avoided all of this if you had only instilled a little more faith in my ability to catch a husband. Reading about such subjects as romance does have its merits. You might try it. I hope for nothing more than for you to experience the joy of falling in love. It is even greater than I had imagined it to be, and that is a great deal indeed.

With love,

Grace

Harriett set her sister's letter down with a sigh, returning her gaze to the plate that lay piled with food before her. She sat alone in the breakfast room as usual. She always arose earlier than her mother and father. There was something about the early morning silence that calmed her. But after reading Grace's letter, she found she was not calm in the slightest.

All the prattle about she and William being well matched was growing tiresome. It had been four days since his accident, and Harriett worried over him constantly. As terrible as it made her sound, she felt the tiniest bit of resentment toward him for going and injuring himself so. It significantly dampened her excitement over her upcoming season. There was also her pending visit to his home, which her uncle insisted on taking her on that very afternoon.

Harriett pushed her plate aside, too nervous to eat a

single bite. She sipped on a glass of lemonade, enjoying the sounds of the early morning from the nearby window. Rose would be joining her for a walk in twenty minutes. Over the last few days, since 'the unfortunate occurrence,' as Rose so vaguely referred to it, Harriett's discussion with her friend had turned from pleasant and light to heavy and depressing. Harriett had been overjoyed to tell Rose of her upcoming season, but it had been overshadowed by talk of William's recovery.

How could she face him today? The thought of entering his home and doting upon him like he was a sick child made her feel quite sick herself. She had been a terrible friend to him over the last nine years. To be so presumptuous as to act as if she were his friend come to check on his well being… it was beyond her capability at the moment. Her palms grew slick with nervous perspiration.

"Me lady." Rebecca's voice severed Harriett's thoughts. "There's a man here to see you."

"A man?" Harriett turned in her chair. Her first thought was William, but it couldn't be him. He must have still been far too out of sorts to be up and about town.

"Yes, miss."

Harriett waited for more details to come flowing from Rebecca's normally loose lips, but nothing came. "Who is he?"

She shrugged one shoulder. "Mr. Radcliffe sent me to convey the message, is all."

Curiosity tugged her to her feet, though they felt glued to the ground with nerves. She had not attended any social events in the last week, so this couldn't be a gentleman calling upon her. Shushing her thoughts and questions, she followed Rebecca out as she led her toward the drawing room. Mr. Radcliffe, the butler, opened the drawing room door for Harriett. She cast him a quizzical look, but he held his lips taut, just as Rebecca had.

Stepping into the room, Harriett's eyes leapt to the gentleman standing, with surprising bearings, near the draperies.

It was William.

Just seeing him here, meeting his green eyes, set her cheeks ablaze. His expression lifted in surprise when he saw her, inquisition, even a hint of admiration. He had never looked at her like that.

She quickly glanced downward, not knowing where else to look. She certainly couldn't look at his eyes, for they were far too familiar and kind and bright. How had he recovered so quickly? For a man who had just nearly died, he appeared more handsome than he deserved.

"You must be Miss Weston." William's voice, a rich and deep sound, vibrated in her ears. Though deepened with age, it was still the same voice, the same inflection and strength as it had carried years before. Distracted as she was by the sound, it took her a moment to recall the words he had spoken. *You must be Miss Weston.*

Must be?

Her eyes lifted, and she stared at him. Was he jesting? He didn't appear to be. She examined the sides of his mouth for any sign of the familiar twitching of a smile. "I—I am," she said, her voice raising at the end, as if it had been a question.

His eyebrows lifted slightly, and he examined her. "You sound uncertain."

Harriett straightened her shoulders, her confusion rising. "No, I am quite certain of who I am." She felt her brow tighten. *But quite uncertain over many other things.*

"What a tremendous feeling that must be." William chuckled softly.

"To be certain of who I am?" She didn't bother hiding her confusion any further.

"Yes." He stepped forward, away from the window. She lowered her gaze to his feet, hoping they would stop in the middle of the room. But instead, they carried him all the way across it, stopping three paces away from her. "That is exactly right."

Harriett was quite certain she had never had such a strange conversation in her life. "I suppose I have never considered a knowledge of my identity to be a tremendous feeling."

"That is because you have never lost it."

Harriett looked up at his face. Awake, William appeared more like the young boy she once knew. His eyes danced, his lips quirked as he spoke, and his expressions were the same as they had been back then, always carrying a hint of mischief.

"Have you...lost it?" she asked.

He nodded. "I scarcely remember anything from my life. Not my family, or my past, and evidently, you."

Understanding pumped through her veins, heavy and slow. "You do not remember me?" As she studied his face, she saw the blankness, the politeness, the reservation of meeting a new acquaintance. Her heart pounded a shallow rhythm.

"I'm afraid not. But the physician did tell me that you saved my life in the woods, and for that I have come to express my immense gratitude. You have likely already been informed, but my name is Mr. William Harrison."

Harriett's breathing had quickened, her stomach growing heavy with dread. She had heard of victims of head injuries losing memories in her brief study of the medical journals in her uncle's extensive library. She swallowed hard, forcing herself to respond. "Yes, I know. We have met, even before the day of your accident."

He took a small step back, his gaze dropping in embarrassment. "Oh. Please forgive me. I have been assured that my memory will most likely return, but as of now it is quite… elusive. My apologies, I must have confused you greatly with my initial greeting. Have we long been acquainted?"

Her mind still reeled, but she managed to stutter out a quick, "Yes."

His eyes met hers. "You do seem rather familiar." He rubbed one side of his head. "But that's how I have felt about everything and everyone in Brighton since I awoke yesterday. Perhaps it means I am on my way to recovering my memories fully." He gave a hopeful smile, one that felt very much like a strike to Harriett's chest.

She took a step back, further widening the space between them. "I hope you recover them swiftly, sir."

"As do I." He hesitated. "I wondered if I may ask a favor of you before I take my leave."

"A favor?" Her voice came out weak.

He stared at her for a long moment before shaking his head softly. "Oh, please forget I said anything. I should not bother you a moment longer."

He offered a bow in farewell, stepping toward the door with purpose in his stride. She couldn't possibly let him leave without knowing what favor he intended to ask of her. William always knew how much she hated when he played games with her curiosity. But this William… he didn't remember that. She had a feeling that if he did indeed remember, however, he would have done so anyway. "Wait—Mr. Harrison." She touched his arm as he passed, quickly retracting her hand when he met her eyes. "What did you mean to ask of me? I am glad to help you." She waited, holding his gaze with great effort.

William looked down at her. He had grown so tall. She had not stood so near to him for nine years, when their heights had been equal, her eyes level with his. But now the top of her head reached only to his nose, leaving her gaze level with his smiling lips. "Miss Weston, you are too kind. You have already saved my life. I couldn't ask another thing of you, for I'm certain I have put you through enough trouble already."

"No, I am in earnest. You cannot leave me to wonder what you meant to ask. Tell me, and then I may determine if it is too much trouble. You have no need to be so gallant with me."

William's eyes sparked with amusement. "A gentleman has need to be gallant with every young lady he meets."

"But you see, we have not just recently met. We have known each other our entire lives." Harriett felt so strange telling William these things that he should have already known.

"An even greater reason to be gallant, for I must give you every reason to wish to continue our acquaintance." He grinned, and Harriett had to look away before she could smile back.

"Well, sir, if you continue to test my patience, I will have a sufficient reason not to continue our acquaintance." She raised one eyebrow at him, hoping he could sense the teasing in her voice.

He laughed, and she had to catch her breath. William's laugh was a sound she hadn't known she had missed so greatly. She had overheard it at various balls and dinners, but she hadn't earned a laugh from him of her own in a very long time.

"Very well," he said. "If you must know, I hoped to ask if you would be willing to help me remember more about my family before they come to visit me this afternoon. You might tell me more about yourself and our abiding friendship as well."

The warmth of his smile, his eyes, and his entire being was troubling beyond what Harriett had expected. Why did it come as such a surprise? If she had cared so much for William as a boy, it was no question that she would be just as affected by William as a man. Even more so. That was likely the reason she had avoided him for so many years. She was quite afraid of him and the way he made her feel. He might stop her from fulfilling her dreams.

Then a memory jarred her mind—the image of frothing white waves, the taste of salt water, and a burning in her lungs—and shocked her out of her thoughts.

"I do not believe I said we were friends," she said in a quick voice. "That is rather a strong word for our relationship. I would say we are well-established acquaintances."

He rubbed his jaw, the smile she had meant to erase only growing wider. "Ah. So we are not friends, but we are not mere acquaintances either?"

She cast her eyes upward. "Yes, I suppose."

"Hmm. I would have judged by the unreserved state of your speech that you are either flippant with social rules, or a close friend of mine. So am I forced to assume the former?"

The teasing in his eyes made her wonder if he was simply jesting about the whole thing—that he did remember her and was simply trying to make her uncomfortable. She eyed him suspiciously. No, this was the William she had known as a child, not the rather stoic, quiet William she had observed at social outings. A realization struck her then. Had his memory of her been what had changed him into such a stoic man? Now that he didn't remember her, his personality had seemed to revert to the way it once had been. To think that she had been the cause of him changing from the lighthearted, teasing boy set her heart aching with regret. She was glad he didn't remember the things she had said to him that day at the ocean.

"I am not flippant with social rules. I am simply… inept." She sighed. "I spend more time scouring the shops of Brighton than learning the correct behavior of a lady in society." She had much to learn in preparation for her season.

Harriett frowned as she thought of one day several years before, when Grace had announced William's departure to London for the season. Jealousy had reared its head in Harriett's young heart, and she had silently prayed he would return unattached. He did. Grace teased her over it, so Harriett had never admitted that she cared, but deep in her heart she had cared very much.

William squinted his eyes, as if studying unseen notations in his mind. He eventually shook his head again, his eyes clearing. "How convenient it must be to remember your own strengths and weaknesses. I wish I remembered. It is the strangest sensation, like grasping at smoke in the air. As a whole, you can see it, muddled and distant. But the moment you grasp onto it, it becomes invisible and intangible." His brow tightened in frustration before he lifted his gaze to hers again. "I find it increasingly bewildering that I could have forgotten you, Miss Weston." He examined her face intently, and she looked away as fast as she could.

A change of subject was in order. "To answer your question from before, I would be happy to help you learn about your family." She left out the part about helping him learn about her. There were too many complicated dealings in their past. She did not wish to explain to him what was already hidden somewhere in his mind, floating around like intangible smoke.

"Thank you," he said, genuine surprise in his features.

She walked to the couch in front of the window, the red velvet curtains hanging halfway open to allow morning sunlight into the room. She made to sit down, but stopped. "Oh! I forgot, I am meeting my friend for a walk. She should be arriving any moment now." She felt a mixture of half relief and half disappointment. Sitting and discussing his memories with him could have counted for her wager with Grace, without even turning into a courtship at all.

He gave a polite smile. "Of course. Take your walk with your friend. I should expect a friend to take precedence of your time over a mere *well-established acquaintance*."

She turned on him, her jaw dropping open slightly. His eyes danced with amusement, and it was all she could do not to slap his arm as she had when they were children when he teased her so mercilessly.

"Miss Harriett. Miss Daventry is here," The butler interrupted. *Drat*. She did not want Rose seeing her in here with William. What was sure to follow from Rose would make William's teasing appear completely novice.

"Please tell her to wait for me in the—" Before she could finish, Rose appeared like a beautiful sunflower behind Mr. Radcliffe, her eyes round and filled with shock as they jumped between Harriett and William. She remained silent for several seconds before taking a step forward.

"Oh! I am sorry to have intruded." Rose threw Harriett a look full of questions. "William! You look so well for a man that has just recently fallen off his horse."

"You have not intruded on anything at all." Harriett

hurried across the room, heart pounding, pulling Rose by the wrist through the doorway. "He does not remember us," she mouthed. Rose only scowled in confusion.

William regarded Rose with a warm smile. "Please remind me of your name. I'm afraid my injuries have rendered me without most of my memory for the time being."

Understanding dawned over Rose's features, and she exchanged a short glance with Harriett before addressing William. "I am very sorry to hear that. How dreadful! I am Miss Rose Daventry. We are well acquainted."

William threw Harriett a sidelong glance before speaking to Rose. "Miss Daventry, would you consider our relationship to be that of friendship?"

"Of course."

His lips twitched as Harriett scowled.

"You must join us on our walk, William," Rose said. "The weather will not hold for long, so we must enjoy it while we can. Harriett would be glad to have you come, wouldn't you, Harriett?" Rose stared at her. Turned away from William's line of sight, she wiggled her eyebrows.

It took all Harriett's concentration not to glare. Rose knew full well that she was going to London soon, that she was not interested in courting William, and that she didn't intend to fulfil her wager with Grace by means of a courtship. So why did she act as if she were playing matchmaker?

When Harriett felt William's gaze on the side of her face, warmer than the sun rays coming through the window, she surrendered. "Yes, we would be glad to have you join us, Mr. Harrison."

In a moment of weakness, she stole a glance at his face. The smile he wore was enough to set her dampened soul on fire.

"And this is the place your horse kicked you in the head," Harriett said. "I don't suppose you remember anything from the accident?" She looked up at William, who stared intently at the forest floor.

"Nothing at all."

Harriett was glad he couldn't recall her leaning her head on his chest, listening to his heartbeat, or brushing the dark hair from his forehead. She shushed her thoughts, concentrating on the even, professional tone of her voice. "The physician and Mr. Daventry then came through the woods and carried you away on a cart in that direction." She pointed east.

William walked in the direction of her finger, his gaze sweeping over the imprints of the cart's wheels that were still visible. He continued walking down the path, and Rose sneaked up and gripped Harriett's arm.

"I cannot believe he does not remember anything," Rose whispered. "The poor man."

Harriett followed Rose's gaze to William's back.

"Although... he does seem to find you every bit as intriguing as he did before." Rose giggled. "Perhaps even more so now that he doesn't remember how you stopped playing with us and quite literally abandoned ship."

Harriet tugged her arm away from her. "Keep your voice down!" she hissed. Rose did not know the worst of what William did not remember from that day.

"He seems rather different." Rose continued to study him. "I was seated next to him at the Miller's soiree just last month, and he was not nearly so... exuberant."

William turned around with a scowl, contradicting

Rose's words. He walked toward them. "I cannot imagine why I was riding so quickly. You said I was bound in that direction?" He pointed the way they had come.

"Yes," Harriett said. "You were riding as if the devil himself were at your heels. You seemed quite intent on your destination, for you did not notice the fallen tree until it was too late. It was so strange. You took me riding once, and—" She stopped herself.

He raised his eyebrows. "I took you riding?"

She didn't know why it made her so flustered, but it was a memory she had cherished for years. To tell William all about it when he should have known it himself made her heart ache. What if he never remembered? A thick knot formed in her throat. "We were very young. But even then, you were quite skilled. I'm certain neither you nor your horse would have missed an obstacle if you hadn't been distracted by something of great importance."

He slid his boot through the dirt, his brow furrowed in apparent thought. "I wish I knew. It would likely bring me a great deal of clarity." He frowned. "Or it would simply result in more confusion."

"It seems only you know the answer." Harriett shrugged. "Or rather, your brain knows the answer, but it is being boorish and keeping it from you."

William laughed, tipping his head back. She smiled, letting the sound soak into her skin, bringing with it memory after memory of what she had abandoned. She had schooled herself into not caring about William, but years of practice were being quickly unraveled. She would need to tread carefully. Her great debut in London society was approaching—she wouldn't let her uncle's generosity go to waste. She had been dreaming since she was little of marrying a duke or marquess or earl. Even a baron would suffice. She had told William so, though he had not liked it very much. That dream was what had led her away from the ocean and back to the house where she could practice the pianoforte and find her rightful and realistic place in the world.

They continued their walk through the woods, and eventually found their way to the public gardens near the royal pavilion, one of the residences of the Prince Regent. The building loomed like a giant before them, the golden stone and indian architecture shining brilliantly under the sun. Spires extended upward, scratching the sky with their menacing points. As they walked, Rose fell behind, first one pace, then two, then ten, until she was simply a shadow, following at a distance like a chaperone. She claimed she wished to enjoy the beautiful scenery in solitude, but Harriett knew her true intentions. *Meddlesome, mischievous girl.*

"As I understand it," William said, "I have an elder brother by the name of Percival, and a sister by the name of Maria."

They walked side by side, at least an arm's length apart. Harriett clasped her hands together in front of her. "Yes. Maria is a dear friend of mine."

She glanced up at him in time to see the right side of his mouth quirk upward. "How is it that she has earned that endearment and I have not?" His voice was innocent, but showed genuine interest.

"Well..." she drew a deep breath. How could she explain it? "If you must know, this morning was the first time you and I have conversed in many years."

His brow creased. "Did I do something to offend you?"

"No." Her curt reply was not enough to convince him.

"I must have done something. Please, tell me so I may apologize."

Harriett looked up at him, at his pleading and sincere eyes. The sight caused guilt to writhe in the pit of her stomach. "I can assure you that you have done nothing wrong."

William stopped walking, taking a pace toward her. "Please, Miss Weston, do not be so mysterious with me. I have enough mystery in my life at the moment already."

"I am not trying to be mysterious."

"Then why don't you tell me what happened?"

She sighed. "Because you will think badly of me." She crossed her arms over her stomach, not enjoying the vulnerability of his interrogation.

"Ah, so it was *you* who did something to offend me." He rubbed his jaw, throwing her a playful smile. He had a voice of authority, but it was gentle at the same time. It was likely a mixture of the old William and the new, the child and the barrister.

"I do not wish to speak about it," she said, hoping her tone was firm enough.

The smile faded from his face and he threw her an inquisitive look. She avoided his eyes for long enough that he dropped the subject, at least for now.

They turned around when they reached the far side of the pavilion, making a circle before heading back in the direction they came. Rose returned to Harriett's side.

"My sister Maria," William continued, "What should I know about her disposition? Is she one that will cry hysterically upon learning that I do not remember her, or will she view it as a minor inconvenience and bear it well?"

"I expect Maria will hold her bearings," Rose piped in, "especially when she learns the physician suspects you will recover your memories."

William chuckled. "Good. And Percival?"

"Oh, Percival will be a watering pot," Harriett said. "He has never contained his emotions well."

They all laughed, and Harriett had the fleeting thought that if Grace were there, it would be just like their childhood, when the four of them had laughed and talked together in such a carefree way.

"What is my father like?" he asked.

Harriett tried to recall what she knew of William's father. He was a quiet man, but a kind one. He was a dear friend of Harriett's father. He had a great deal of patience, she could only assume, for he was married to a woman that would require it in spades. "I expect your father is still on the hunting trip that you departed early from. He is a very good man, and you love him very much."

"And my mother?"

Harriett and Rose exchanged a glance. Mrs. Harrison was as any mother should be—protective of her children—but to a fault. She had an abiding hatred for Harriett, one that she took no care in concealing. "Your mother loves you very much," Harriett said. She opened her mouth to say more, but closed it again. She tried to think of something else to say, but she had been taught not to speak ill of anyone.

William's eyes grew bright with wonder. "How strange it will be to see my family as if I am meeting them for the first time. I look forward to it."

She admired his positivity in light of such a horrible situation. She couldn't imagine what it would be like to forget her family. She loved them all dearly.

"But surely it will be even more strange from their perspective," he continued. "For example, if I were to meet you tomorrow and you did not remember me, I would be quite put out."

It took Harriett a moment to realize that Rose had once again faded into the background, leaving her alone with William. He stared down at her—she could feel it—but she continued looking straight ahead. "Do not worry, Mr. Harrison. I am not nearly as careless of a rider as you."

He laughed. Little did William know that she had been trying to forget him for years. It would certainly not happen overnight, even if she wanted it to. Silence fell between them for a long moment as they walked through the trees, following the path they had taken toward the pavilion.

"I would like to hear about this ride I took you on," William said. His voice was hesitant, as if he had been carefully planning the request in that long moment of silence.

She shifted uncomfortably. Considering how many years that had passed since that ride, he would think it was strange how many details she remembered. If she hadn't spent so many hours reflecting on it, she might have forgotten the minute ones. But even now, nine years later, she remembered every detail. She had tucked each away as a precious memory, untouched in her heart. She hadn't reflected on it for years, but now, with William's closeness and voice and smile, it all came pouring back like sun-warmed honey.

Chapter 6

NINE YEARS BEFORE

The day was as hot as any summer day, yet Harriett's cheeks felt much warmer than usual. She peered out the back window of the house where the sun beat down through the glass, watching William as he approached from the woods that joined their two houses. Grace had claimed she was too ill to join them, but Harriett suspected she had simply pretended so as to put her sister in this awkward situation. For a girl of ten, Grace was quite devious.

Harriett took a deep breath. If her parents knew that she was planning to take her first riding lesson from a fourteen year old boy, they would be fit to be tied. They knew William was a skilled rider, especially for his young age, but she doubted they would trust him to teach her. The Harrisons stabled many fine horses, and William had assured *both Harriett and Grace that they had many gentle mares for them to practice with. The idea sent Harriett's stomach into a whirlwind, but more troubling than that were the feelings that had begun to make manifest in her heart. The feelings stirred and jumped at the sight of William crossing the grass, a wide smile on his face.*

Harriett ducked below the window before standing up again. She could not let him see that she had been spying.

She walked through the back door and met William on the lawn. His smile dropped a little when he saw her. "What is the matter?"

"Grace isn't coming. She does not feel well."

"I suppose you will simply be forced to have more attention from your instructor."

"I told you I do not like horses." She shifted on her feet, fiddling with the buttons on her riding habit. "We should postpone the lesson to another day when Grace can come."

William shook his head. "If you wish to beat Grace in the jousting tournament tomorrow, you must gain some experience on horseback. Riding an imaginary horse is very similar to riding a real one, you know."

She laughed as they started walking toward the woods. "No, that cannot be true. I suspect riding an imaginary horse is much easier."

He shrugged. "You cannot say for certain, for you lack experience in both. I have ridden both real and imaginary horses, and I can promise that it is very similar."

She gave him a skeptical look. "You are teasing me."

"No, I am not. You must be imagining that."

"But surely real teasing and imaginary teasing are very similar."

"Not as similar as riding real and imaginary horses."

Harriett suppressed her grin with a thoughtful expression.

"But you cannot fall off an imaginary horse. You cannot be hurt by one."

"That is true, but where is the thrill in that?" William grinned at her as they approached the property line of his home. Harriett knew her family owned the land directly beside the Harrison's property. It was a long, wide stretch of dead, patchy grass, complete with gnarled trees. Her family used it for nothing. They did not want it or need it, but could not seem to sell it. Harriett and William had once pretended it was a magical forest filled with witches and goblins. Leaping over the ugly mounds of vegetation, they raced to the stables. William won, of course. He always did.

When they walked through the wooden doors, the strong scents of animals made Harriett's nose wrinkle. The stables were quiet. She had never expected horses to be so quiet and calm, but here they were, rows and rows of them, peacefully munching on oats behind their stalls.

"I have decided to start you on a pony," William said, gesturing at a very small horse in a nearby stall.

She shook her head hard, her blond curls whipping over her face. "No. If I am to be prepared for an imaginary joust with Grace, I will need to practice with a much larger steed." She paused, tapping her chin. "Larger, but still gentle."

He grinned "I know the perfect one. She is fifteen hands, quite large, but she is also very gentle. She used to be my father's horse, but he gave her to me. She loves apples more than any other horse I know, and also sugar. I don't ride her often anymore. I am fairly certain she prefers female riders, so you shall be the perfect fit." His eyes sparked with excitement and affection as he spoke. Harriett had never known that he loved his animals so much.

He led her to a stall on the opposite side of the stables, pausing in front of a large horse with coffee colored eyes and *a coat the color of dry sand.* "You will like her very much," he said.

"It does not matter if I like her." Harriett swallowed. "I would much rather she like me."

He laughed. "She would be a fool not to like you."

Harriett's eyes jumped to his face in time to see a blush steal across his freckled cheeks. He looked away fast, returning his attention to the horse. "I have asked one of our grooms to assist us today. He will prepare the horses and help you mount."

Harriett nodded, her fear dissipating as she stared into the horse's large brown eyes. It did seem to be a gentle, sweet horse, after all.

William led her outside where they stood near the stable doors, waiting for the groom to bring the horses out. She bounced up and down on her feet. "What is it like to ride a horse? Tell me the truth, William."

"It is like… flying, but much closer to the ground. It makes you feel so powerful and strong and courageous. Each time I ride I vow that I will never stop feeling such things, but the moment I dismount the feeling disappears. Only horses can bring such courage."

She frowned. "That cannot be true, William. You are the most courageous boy I know. You fight wicked pirates and sea creatures. I have never met another boy that can do that."

He laughed. "Yes, but I am not that courageous with other things."

"What other things?"

He shifted on his feet. "Nothing."

"You must tell me now, William. You know how I despise being curious."

He stared at her, his eyes full of secrets that made her all the more curious. He shook his head.

"Please, William! At least tell me what it is about. I simply cannot imagine you being afraid of anything." She bounced up and down again.

He sighed. "Very well. It's about a girl I fancy."

She stopped, suddenly much less curious than she had been before. Her heart pounded. She did not wish to hear about a girl William fancied and how he was too afraid to tell her. Jealousy leapt like a flame inside her, bringing two circles of heat to her cheeks. "Oh. Well, you do not need to learn to be courageous in those sort of matters, William. You are still far too young to begin courting, and that is when you will need to have courage, not now."

He laughed, the sound more shy than it usually was. "I suppose you are right." She followed his gaze as the groom brought the horses out of the stables toward them. "You would never wish to court me anyway."

Harriett's eyes jumped back to his face, but he didn't look at her. His smile implied that he was teasing, but the color of his cheeks did not.

He said nothing more on the subject as they approached the horses, and Harriett found herself more curious than she had ever been in her entire life. Yet she knew enough to refrain from questioning William further, for she had seen all the answers in his eyes. Why did William think she would never wish to court him? She had never said as much. At her age, she had never given any thought to courting, but if she had to imagine herself all grown up and courting anyone, it would certainly be William.

The groom helped her mount, and she gripped the pommel of her saddle with all her strength. Her knuckles turned white with the effort. She peered down at the grass, and it seemed much farther away than she had anticipated. William had said that riding felt like flying close to the ground, but she felt as if she were all the way up in the clouds. Her heart began racing with panic.

"You lied to me!" she blurted.

William cast her a look of confusion.

"You said riding a real horse was like riding an imaginary one."

His lips twitched. "That depends on the strength of your imagination."

Harriett's imagination was not weak, but her stomach was becoming increasingly so. The groom held her horse's reins as its legs began moving. She bobbed up and down like the waves of the sea, and she clutched the pommel tighter. "I cannot do it!"

"Yes, you can," William said. "Try to feel courageous and powerful like I said you would."

She stared at the land ahead, imagining it was a raging battleground and she was leading her army to victory. Her posture straightened and the stabbing fear in her stomach lessened with each sedate step of her horse. She laughed. "It isn't so very bad."

He smiled from his place atop his dark brown horse. "You can achieve anything with enough courage."

She tucked the words, along with his bright smile, away in her heart, to a place where she would always remember them. She couldn't wait to tell Rose and Grace that she had ridden a horse. With William as an ally, she was sure to win the jousting tournament. She was sure to win anything she ever wanted.

※

"It was as ordinary as any ride could be," Harriett said. She pushed away the tingling sensation that had spread over her skin, the belonging and hope that had entered her heart from the memory. "All except for the fact that I was being taught by a fourteen year old boy."

William's eyes rounded in delight, another expression that reminded her of the younger version of him. "That could not have been a wise decision."

She shook her head, a slight smile pulling on the corners of her mouth. "You were a surprisingly adept teacher." She continued walking in silence, the heat of William's gaze beating down on the side of her face.

"Is that all you intend to tell me about it?" he asked.

"Yes, I'm afraid that is all I remember."

He eyed her with suspicion. "I'm not certain I believe that claim. I think you are simply attempting once again to be mysterious."

"I am not," Harriett stepped over a loose branch on the path.

"I believe you are. But no matter. I will allow you to continue your little mystery. I'm certain I will be able to solve it all quite easily once my memories return."

She swallowed, the action bringing attention to her dry throat. "Yes, so you have no need to question me further." She smiled, but it came off forced.

He was still studying her, and she had the urge to push him away from her and call to Rose to come join them. Her friend had increased her distance to at least ten feet, pretending to have intense interest in the trees they passed. Harriett was certain Rose was simply trying to appear nonchalant with her eavesdropping. There was no question she was listening to every word.

Within seconds, they came out of the woods and onto the back property of Weston Manor. William continued asking questions about his family, to which Harriett easily replied, except when he inquired after his mother. She still had little to say about the woman, at least little *good* to say. Even so, Harriett much preferred conversation that didn't involve herself and how she had left him by the ocean those years ago. If it was true, that William would soon recover his memories, then she had no need to explain. He would remember soon enough. And how could she explain? She did not fully understand how her words and actions had affected him these years. He could very well have taken it as lightly as she hoped he had.

"This has been a pleasure." William offered her a wide smile as he turned to face her. Rose approached tentatively behind, coming to a stop at Harriett's side.

"I am glad you were able to join us, Mr. Harrison," Rose said.

"As am I. I will speak with my family this evening, and based on your endorsements of their characters, I will assume they will be happy to receive both your families for dinner next week."

"That would be delightful!" Rose spoke far too enthusiastically. She threw her wide-eyed gaze at Harriett. "Won't it, Harriett?"

Amid the twisting in her stomach, she almost forgot to answer. "Yes." Her voice came out bleak. She could only assume that Mrs. Harrison would be quite chagrined at the suggestion. There was no way to explain it without being rude, so she simply said, "I wish you all the best in your meeting with your family, Mr. Harrison. I'm certain you will like them very much."

"I have no doubt. From what I have already discovered from my past, I have found there is much to like."

Harriett didn't dare look up at him again. From the masked gasp of delight that came from Rose, she could only guess William was looking at Harriett.

"Good day Miss Weston, Miss Daventry."

Harriett gave a polite nod as William dismissed himself from the property.

The moment he was out of sight, Rose leapt into the air with a twirl, causing her bonnet to come loose. She giggled, wrapping Harriett's arm up tightly with her own. "I knew you two were the perfect match. Grace has been right all this time."

Harriett tried to pull her arm out of Rose's grasp, but she was too weak. "No, we are not the perfect match. I am going to find my perfect match in London, don't you remember?"

Rose gave an exasperated sigh. "Oh, Harriett. You are so very blind."

"I am not blind. I am rational. If I were to stay here and court William when he has no memory of what I did to drive him away, then it would not be fair to him at all. At any rate, it would be pathetically unwise to toss aside the opportunity that my uncle is providing me with, and I cannot bear to disappoint him or my parents. I'm certain Grace will understand and let me out of my wager. Until then, I will continue to be a… good friend to William and help him through his difficult time. Once he recovers his memory, I'm certain he, as well as I, will wish never to see the other again."

Rose stared at her blankly. "What happened between you and William?"

Harriett squeezed her eyes shut. "I spoke too freely, and so did he."

"What did you say?"

Harriett sighed. She did not wish to speak of it. She had spent far too much time already dwelling on it in the last several days. "Something I deeply regret. But I cannot take it back, not even now that William does not remember. That would not be fair."

Rose looked as if she wanted to inquire further but decided against it. It seemed she wasn't quite as curious as Harriett was. "If you can find a man in London that looks at you the way William looks at you, then I suppose I will be satisfied."

"He doesn't look at me in any special way." Harriett scoffed.

"He does, and you don't even realize it." Rose took three steps before a smile curled her lips. "But will you ever look at any other man the way you look at William? I cannot imagine it to be possible."

Harriett considered denying it, but instead scowled at the ground as they made their way to the house. At least one good thing had become of this day. She had now completed her first meeting with William. Only two remained before she could be free of him, and her wager, forever.

Chapter 7

William had fully expected to like his family, but what he hadn't expected was for his mother to have an abiding dislike of Miss Harriett Weston.

"Well, I adore Miss Weston," his sister Maria said. "She and I share many of the same interests. We both enjoy artistic pastimes such as painting and sketching and decorating bonnets. I find no fault in her." Maria sat on the settee dressed in an elegant ivory gown. They were awaiting their guests, the Daventrys and Westons, the latter of the families grudgingly invited by his mother. William had yet to see his father, who was still at the hunting lodge, intent to finish his trip.

William leaned against the pianoforte. His mind was still as muddled as it had been a week before when he had regained consciousness, and even more so since meeting his family.

"I do not like her," his mother said.

William turned toward her, where she sat on the brocade sofa in the far corner of the room. Her eyes sparked with vehement distaste, her dark hair shrouding the expression. William raised his eyebrows. "You have not given me your reason for disliking her. I found her to be quite agreeable. She spoke kindly of you. I sensed no feud between the two of you."

His mother sighed. "The feud is not between herself and I. She broke your young heart, William. I cannot respect her for that. If you remembered the circumstances, then you would despise her as much as I do."

"Do not listen to Mama," Maria whispered. "You do not hold such ill feelings toward Miss Weston. In fact—"

"Oh, no, no, Maria." His mother sat forward. "You did not see the way she affected him like I did. Miss Weston is—"

William held up a hand to stop her. "Perhaps I should decide for myself how I feel about Miss Weston. I do not need you all telling me how I should think and feel. Miss Weston will be arriving soon, and please do not forget that she saved my life. Do treat her with respect and kindness or I will be tempted to alter my opinions of you in the way you have tried to alter my opinion of her." He sighed, rubbing a circle over his temple.

Maria fidgeted in her seat, looking up at William with pleading eyes. He met her gaze, offering an apologetic look. His words had been intended wholly for his mother, not his sister. Of all the members of his family that he had become reacquainted with so far, Maria was quickly becoming his favorite. But of all the people he had become reacquainted with, Miss Weston was the only one he could not seem to rid his mind of. She felt the most familiar, as if her influence on his life had been the greatest. He had enjoyed his time with her more than he had anyone else. But she, much like his family, had been keeping secrets from him. He was determined to discover what they were.

"Ah, I see a carriage is arriving on the drive." His mother craned her neck, a dissatisfied smirk on her lips. "The Weston's carriage, I believe. It always was a shabby one."

William looked out the window behind him and watched as a woman that appeared to be his mother's age descended, then a man, and then Miss Weston. He caught his breath as she smiled at the footman, taking his hand and landing softly on her feet.

"Step away from the window, William. You may frighten her." Maria laughed. He took a seat beside his sister. She leaned toward him with a whisper. "Did you read the letter I sent to the hunting lodge?"

"Letter?" He watched as the drawing room door opened. He stood.

"Yes," Maria whispered. "It was addressed to me, but the sender requested that I forward it to your address. I thought you would have read it."

William shook his head, distracted by the entrance of their guests. "No. I received nothing."

The footman introduced Mr. and Mrs. Weston, then their daughter. Miss Weston stepped into the room, her lips pressed together, and her cheeks flushed at the centers. Her fingers fiddled with the fabric of her blue skirts as her eyes swept over everything in the room. Everything except William.

His mother welcomed their guests to the house, her courtesy toward Mr. and Mrs. Weston no match for the glare she cast in their daughter's direction. William's jaw tightened when his mother approached Miss Weston with a brief nod, her lips still curled in a smirk of disapproval. Percival greeted the party, and William and Maria followed suit.

"Miss Weston," William said, nodding deeply. "I am glad you were able to come this evening."

She raised her eyes to his for the length of a blink before lowering them to the ground once again. He was fairly certain that if he could look in her eyes for long enough, he might be able to remember every lost thought that pertained to her. But she insisted on looking away after the briefest glance. Was she intimidated by his family? The way she held her posture and expression suggested that she was nervous. He couldn't blame her. He watched his mother, intending to step in front of her if she attempted one more barbed glance.

"Thank you for the invitation," Miss Weston said in a small voice.

The Daventrys entered behind the Westons, and William moved forward to greet them. While his back was turned, his mother determined it was time to enter the drawing room, ushering Miss Weston onto Percival's arm before William could escort her. William guided Miss Daventry to the dining room instead, his vexation growing when his mother seated Miss Weston on the opposite side of the table, as far as possible from him.

The first course was brought in, and the conversation broke into sections of the table. Miss Weston, her parents, Percival, and Maria sat on one end. William caught pieces of the conversation, but not enough to take part in it. His side of the table consisted of his mother and the Daventrys, who also had two young boys.

"I hear you are recently engaged to Sir Martin Gouldsmith," His mother said to Miss Daventry.

"I am."

"Oh, what a lovely match." She turned to Mr. and Mrs. Daventry. "Are you quite pleased with your daughter's selection?"

"Indeed, we are. Sir Martin is an amiable, honest, and kind man, the only thing that would suit our Rose."

William's mother laughed, a light, airy sound. "Of course. I expect nothing short of such a match for my children as well."

He sensed the warning behind his mother's words, but he couldn't help but look across the table at Miss Weston. She appeared every bit as uncomfortable as she had before. Her eyes found his for a short moment before flitting away.

When the meal was finished and the group had removed to the drawing room, William made sure to find a seat nearby Miss Weston before his mother could make other arrangements.

"Let us play a game of whist!" she exclaimed the moment the rest of the men entered the room. "My William adores playing whist." She eyed the card table pointedly, attempting to beckon William forward from his seat. He studied Miss Weston's profile as she carefully avoided his gaze. If he had any hope of discovering her secrets, he would need to speak with her tonight.

"Come, come, William, join us in our game." His mother sat down at the card table, ushering him over with a bit more force. "Who would like to be William's partner?" She fixed her gaze on Miss Daventry. "Come, Miss Daventry. I suspect you are quite skilled at the game."

She stepped tentatively forward, glancing at Miss Weston before leaving her side and sitting down at the table.

"There is room at the other table for two more players." His mother gestured at the card table where Mr. and Mrs. Weston sat. Mr. and Mrs. Daventry quickly took up the chairs. Percival sat in the corner with a book, and Maria sat nearby, watching the card table arrangements attentively.

"Now, William, come join your partner." His mother's eyes did not leave room for negotiation, but he intended to argue anyway.

"I'm afraid I do not recall how to play whist what with my injuries," he said in a voice of false disappointment. "I should hate to slow your game. Please proceed without me. I'm certain Maria would like to join Miss Daventry, and Percival could be your partner this round."

Maria jumped out of her seat without a moment of hesitation. "Yes, Mama. I would love to join your game. Rose and I are quite skilled at whist. I daresay we will provide a great deal of competition to you and Percival."

With a sigh, Percival set down his book, whisked his spectacles off his nose, and joined his mother at the table. William watched the growing distress on his mother's face with masked amusement. What was so dangerous about Miss Weston? His mother let out a puff of air, throwing a masked frown in William's direction. He smiled to himself as she dealt the cards, her brow still creased at the center.

The Daventry boys had taken to reading a book in the place Percival had been sitting, leaving Miss Weston and William to speak without interruption. He leaned toward her across the armrest of his chair. The moment he did, however, she stood, walking toward the adjacent wall where two paintings hung. By the abrupt nature of her departure, he could only guess that he made her nervous. He needed to understand why.

He caught his mother's disapproving eye before standing up. He followed Miss Weston to the painting, a depiction of Brighton that she had begun studying intently. He stopped just behind her left shoulder. Her posture visibly tightened.

"What do you think of the painting?" he asked, making sure to keep his voice low so his mother wouldn't overhear.

She turned slightly toward him, but once again refused to meet his eyes for longer than a brief moment. "It is beautiful. I have never seen such an accurate depiction of Brighton." She leaned close to the lower right corner of the painting, seemingly examining the initials there.

"Thank you," William said.

"Did you paint this?" She turned around, her expression filled with surprise. With the blue of the ocean behind her in the painting, combined with the blue of her gown, the color of her eyes was striking.

"I am told that I did." He chuckled. "Although I do not remember painting it."

She returned her attention to the brushstrokes, touching her fingers softly against the frame. "You must have spent weeks on it."

He studied the painting again, just as he had days before when his mother had told him he was the creator of it. He still couldn't believe that he had applied the even strokes, mixed the deep and stunning colors, or had the eye of accuracy that Miss Weston had noted. Staring at the painting now felt like he was admiring someone else's work, not his own. He wanted to praise it the way Miss Weston did, but to do so would be appear extremely prideful. He felt he could have no ownership over something so beautiful.

"For me to have created something like this, I must have spent a great deal of time. I hope to take another attempt at painting this week to discover if I have lost my talent for it."

She nodded eagerly, her gaze landing on his again. "Yes, you should. This is breathtaking. I doubt you could ever lose a talent such as this."

He held her gaze, searching for answers within it. He felt close to grasping something, but he didn't yet understand what it was. "My mother told me, with great disdain, that I climbed a tree to attain the correct vantage point."

Miss Weston gave a quiet laugh. "Yes, it appears you painted from the woods between our homes to achieve this angle of the ocean."

She glanced upward at the top left corner, where a modest home sat near the sea. "Is that my family's home?"

He squinted. "It appears so." He realized that besides the ocean, Weston Manor was the only main focus of the painting. The colors blurred around the scenery between the water, horizon, and Weston Manor, with the house being the most prominent landmark.

She rotated abruptly, coming to face him again. "I'm curious. Did you really forget how to play whist?"

A slow smile pulled on his lips. He tried to suppress it, but he failed miserably. "I suppose I could probably recall most of the rules."

Miss Weston's features scrunched together in confusion. "Why then did you refuse to play?"

"Because *you* were not invited to play." He gave a soft smile, one that caused her to look down at her gloves. He lowered his voice. "My mother has it in her mind that I should not converse with you, or be near you for that matter. In fact, as we speak, she is likely staring daggers into the back of my head."

Miss Weston's eyes traveled over his shoulder. "She is indeed." A soft laugh escaped her, but she raised a hand to stifle it. "Though I think daggers is too mild a word. Swords would be more accurate. At any rate, they are directed more at me than you."

He gave her a look of mock warning. "You mustn't let her see you smile. She will become far too suspicious of us and quit her game altogether."

Miss Weston straightened her mouth and set her eyebrows. "Is this better?"

He laughed. "Yes, but she will likely find fault in that expression as well. She is quite determined to hate you."

The playful expression on Miss Weston's face vanished, her gaze dropping. "She has a very good reason to hate me."

William studied the downtrodden expression on her face. He couldn't name the look in her eyes. Was it regret? Anger? Resentment? Her gaze found his again, tentative, uncertain.

"What reason could that be?" he asked.

"To put it simply, I was not nearly as kind to you as you were to me." She shook her head ruefully.

"That is not a good reason. No one could possibly be as kind as me," he teased.

As if by great effort, she smiled. "You are right. All you ever were was kind, and I am very grateful to have had you as my friend."

"And now? Would you venture to call me your friend? Or am I still a mere acquaintance?"

She was silent for a long moment, turning back toward the painting. "I suspect you were always my friend, but I was not always yours. For that, I apologize."

He joined her in her study of the painting, wondering if her appreciation for it was genuine, or if she was simply trying to avoid his gaze. "I accept your apology, even if I do not know exactly what it is for."

She turned around, her pretty eyes open in surprise.

"It does not matter what happened in the past," he said. "I am realizing that now more than ever. What matters is what we do with the time ahead of us, and the time all around us. Right now, I'm choosing to admire this painting with you. Tomorrow, I would like to invite you to join me in my pursuit of my old artistic talents."

"I beg your pardon?"

"I would like to invite you to join me as I attempt to paint again." He waited, watching her signs of unrest with growing curiosity.

"Well—er... I suppose... yes."

He grinned as color rose to her cheeks. He couldn't imagine feeling anything but delight in her company. What had passed between them? Part of him was afraid to discover what it was, but the other was unendingly curious.

"I will look forward to it." He smiled down at Miss Weston. She hesitated before smiling back. His heart flipped, stirring with emotions that were both new and familiar.

"We have won!" His mother's voice called him back to the present, the details of the room returning to focus. She threw her cards down on the table in triumph, turning to her eldest son. "Percival, I am quite surprised you managed to win so many tricks."

He gave a deep chuckle. "I was quite splendid, was I not?"

"Indeed! William, won't you join us for the next

round?" His mother's invitation held every undertone of a threat.

"No, thank you, mother. I am quite content to remain here with Miss Weston. We are studying the paintings."

Her nostrils flared as a huffed breath escaped her. She didn't speak a word as she dealt her cards, at least not verbally. But the narrowed slits of her eyes and the set of her jaw spoke much more than any words could have.

William turned around, his laughter throbbing in his chest. Miss Weston met his eyes, her lips twitching. "I suspect you will be receiving a firm scolding later this evening," she whispered.

He released the reins on his laughter, the sound much louder than he intended. He cleared his throat. "I do not doubt it. Do you recall if I was this rebellious before the accident?"

She tapped her chin. "As a child you often defied your mother, but only in innocent matters."

He raised his eyebrows. "Is this not innocent? How dangerous could it be studying a painting with you, Miss Weston?" He realized he had leaned closer as he spoke.

"Not much more dangerous than playing a game of whist, I'd wager."

He glanced behind him where his mother and Percival had taken up their new game with ferocity, slapping their cards down with great force. He threw his head back with a laugh. "I think you are right."

She shifted her gaze to the portrait beside the Brighton painting, turning away from him once again. "Who is this?" She gave a shy smile, glancing up through her lashes. "If you remember."

He looked up at the tall, regal man in the portrait. He had a thick mustache and full cheeks, with a long, pointed nose and large ears. William didn't know precisely who was in the painting, only that it was a very odd looking man. The man reminded him of something, but he could not quite place the image. "I'm not certain," he said. "But he looks rather strange, does he not?" His voice caught on the laughter he was trying to suppress.

Miss Weston nodded respectfully, her eyes examining the portrait. "Yes, but I do see a slight resemblance to you."

He threw his gaze at her. "You cannot be serious."

"Not in the ears or the nose, I assure you. I see a similarity in your eyes. His are green, just like yours, with dark lashes and a certain brightness and joy within them. Optimism and hope." She took one long look at the painting again before her gaze traveled to William's face.

"An elephant," he blurted as the answer came to him. "This man resembles an elephant, and so do I, it seems."

She burst into laughter.

"I recall learning about elephants at school," he said. "You see? His skin has a certain leathery, gray quality as well."

Miss Weston covered her mouth, her eyes filled with amusement as she stared at the elephant-man's face in the portrait.

William leaned close to her, picking up the scent of roses. "Please assure me that I do not remind you of an elephant."

She sighed, her laughter subsiding. "I assure you, you are much more handsome than that." The moment the words escaped, her eyes widened, and her cheeks colored.

He grinned. "And you too are much more handsome than an elephant."

She covered half her face, falling into laughter once again. "I should hope so."

William felt a firm tap on the back of his shoulder. He

turned to see his mother, a tempest brewing in her eyes as she watched their exchange. "Are you making a mockery of your grandfather?"

Ah. It was his *grandfather*. William shook his head fast. "No, not at all. Miss Weston and I were simply admiring his exotic qualities." Miss Weston's laughter had halted beside him, and he stole a glance at her face. She stared at his mother with wide, innocent eyes.

"William, what has happened to you?" His mother's voice lowered. "Ever since you awoke from your dreadful head injury, you have been acting the part of a fool. You have become disrespectful, disinterested in the company of my guests, and jovial to the point of excess. I have not seen you behave in such a manner since you were a child."

He felt his cheeks growing hot, a sensation he likely hadn't felt since he was a child. The entire room had turned their gazes toward him and his mother, discreetly listening behind their cards. Even the young Daventry boys in the corner had set their book down, watching the exchange with furrowed brows.

"Mother," William began in a quiet voice, "Please understand that none of this is my intention. I do not remember how I behaved before falling off my horse. I do not know what I liked and what I disliked, or whose company I chose to keep. Since waking up the only things that have been clear to me are that I quite enjoy being *excessively* jovial, I do not enjoy being forced to do things I do not wish to do, and I am quite content in the company of Miss Weston, even if you are not."

His mother's lower lip quivered as she surveyed him, the sadness in her eyes shocking. "I do hope you remember soon the things that are most important to you. Miss Weston has not been among them since you were a child.

I have been." With that she turned around, rushing toward the card table to finish her game. The room had fallen silent, and Miss Weston had taken to staring at the ground once again.

William's face burned. He turned toward Miss Weston, intending to apologize, but she slipped away, moving to a chair across the room. He remained by the paintings, left to wonder, yet again, what Miss Weston had done to earn such disdain from his mother.

Chapter 8

"I believe at least four new ball gowns are in order for your season," Harriett's mother said. They sat in the drawing room of Weston Manor, with Harriett's father at the writing desk across the room. Much to Harriett's dismay, she was rather disinterested in her mother's talk of ball gowns. "The modiste in Worthing is preferable, so we shall take our business to her. Cornelius has written up the estimated costs of your season, so we will soon know what we have to work with."

Harriett looked down at the fashion plates on the coffee table. A spark of excitement flickered in her chest but was quickly stamped out when she remembered the dinner party the night before. How awkward the entire evening had been! She had known that Mrs. Harrison disliked her, but had never seen her show it in such a public manner. Harriett's parents had been upset at first over the woman's behavior toward their daughter, but their anger had been quickly stamped out when Papa received a letter from William's father that morning.

Her father glanced up from his desk, scooting his chair out to face them. Mr. Weston was a formidable, robust man at first glance, towering much taller than most of his acquaintances, but Harriett knew him to be gentle and kind beneath it all. She and Grace had often laughed over the idea of their father scaring away any unwanted suitors they might encounter.

He smiled broadly, turning toward his wife. "My dear, Mr. Harrison has just expressed most enthusiastically that he would like to purchase a portion of our land—the wooded area bordering their property—and many of our stallions. I hardly ride anymore and do not travel far, so they are not needed. I always knew their bloodline to be greater than they are given credit, but could never convince a single buyer of their merit. That is, until Mr. Harrison made me this offer."

Mrs. Weston gasped. "You cannot be serious! That is wonderful news! Do you mean that ugly, patchy stretch just past the knoll near our gardens? That would give them plenty of space to build their larger stables."

"Precisely. The portion he intends to pay for both the property and the horses will pay off what remains of our debts." Mr. Weston's deep voice wavered with emotion as his wife came to stand behind him. She squeezed his hand, her own smile even larger than it had been when she was speaking of gowns. Mr. Weston dropped the letter on the desk, standing up to embrace her. "We will be free at last."

"That is wonderful news, Papa!" Harriett jumped to her feet, meeting her parents across the room. Her dampened spirits and ill opinion toward the Harrisons vanished as she saw her father's elevated mood. Tears sprung to his normally placid expression, and she hugged him.

"It is indeed," he said. "We might have sent you to London without the help of Cornelius at this rate." He chuckled, and Harriett practically felt the weight of his burden melting away as she hugged him. "I always knew Mr. Harrison was a good man."

Harriett had scarcely seen her parents so happy. The financial burden that had weighed upon them was much more noticeable now that it was gone. Their eyes carried a new light, their posture more confident, and their smiles unconquerable. Surely Uncle Cornelius had offered to assist them financially many times, but her parents had been selfless enough to turn him down if it meant the money could go to Harriett's dream of having a season. It ached her to think that her parents had wanted to send her to London for so long, but had been unable to afford it. Everything was made right now, though, and the joy in the drawing room was tangible.

"Now, do not let me interrupt your fun," her father said to his wife. "Continue planning for Harriett's season."

Her mother turned, squealing with delight. "Oh, what a wonderful day this is turning out to be. Despite Mrs. Harrison's unacceptable behavior yesterday evening, she has regained a portion of my respect."

There was little that could dampen Harriett's positive mood like a reminder of the evening before. She sat down on the sofa with her mother, who took her hand tenderly. "I did not have a season when I was young, so you know how this planning excites me." She clasped her hands together. "We must begin soon with practicing your behavior and etiquette. After what I witnessed last night, I expect there are many improvements to be made."

"Last night?" Harriett had hoped her mother hadn't noticed any faults in her behavior. "What about last night?"

"You know perfectly well."

"I confess, I do not." Harriett tried to hold still, keeping her gaze fixed innocently on her mother's. It didn't work.

"Oh, Harriett. The painting of William's grandfather was only the start of the issue. There was your refusal to play whist, your lack of interesting conversation, and the way you secluded yourself to a corner with William. One in attendance might have suspected there was an attachment between the two of you."

Harriett frowned. "I was not invited to play whist. William simply took pity on me for his mother's lack of inclusion."

Her mother huffed a breath. "That was quite rude of her, wasn't it? What have you done to have her hate you so very much? She is a crass and disagreeable woman if I have ever met one, although I cannot hate her so much after we received her husband's letter this morning."

"What might I have done to improve my behavior?"

"You might have avoided encouraging William. By laughing and teasing with him in the corner of the room you drew a great deal of attention. In London, if a man is interested in you but is not a desirable match, you must deter his attention from the very first sign of it. Men take the slightest smile or glance as encouragement, and you had plenty of those for the young Mr. Harrison last night."

Dread pooled in Harriett's stomach. She had not meant to encourage him, and yet she still had. Grace's wager had required her to meet with him three times and encourage him into a courtship—was she fulfilling the second part of the wager without even realizing it? She could count the dinner party as her second meeting with William, so she only had one remaining. She had escaped so far without creating a courtship out of their time spent together. Surely William wouldn't try to court her without having his memories back... would he? He had every reason not to trust her after witnessing his mother's hatred for her.

Harriett told herself not to worry, but a small part of her doubted the strength of her heart's resolve in avoiding William after her wager was complete. It was pathetically stupid of her. Once he knew her true nature, recalled the things she had said and done, he would remember why he kept his distance for so many years. He would remember how much he hated her.

Her heart stung at the thought. She banished it as quickly as she could. She could not change the past, no matter how much she wanted to.

"Let us practice," her mother said. "If a gentleman that is not suitable for marriage meets your eyes across an assembly room, what should you do to immediately deter him? Please demonstrate."

Harriett's mother, who she assumed was pretending to be the undesirable gentleman, had straightened her posture, glancing about the room lazily. Her gaze connected with Harriett's, lingering there for several seconds. Harriett looked away fast, casting her eyes down to the floor.

"No, no, no, definitely not." Her mother stood, taking a deep and collective breath. She raised a finger at Harriett, emphasizing each word with a wag of her finger. "You must never look down when glancing away from a gentleman that you wish to deter. Looking down will convey shyness and come across as an attempt to be coy and flirtatious. He will assume that you are playing games with him and would like to be introduced."

Harriett thought of the night before at the Harrison's, how she had repeatedly glanced at the floor when speaking with William. Her cheeks burned. Where else was she supposed to look when she was trying to avoid his much-too-handsome green eyes? She hadn't meant to encourage him by glancing down at her gloves or the floor. She had meant to hide, or perhaps avoid the feelings his gaze sent spiraling through her heart.

"Try again." Her mother flicked her wrist, shifting her gaze to Harriett in the method of the pretend-gentleman. Harriett met her eyes for a brief moment before turning her gaze upward and sliding it away in an exasperated manner. What her mother would not know was that the exasperation was entirely genuine.

"No! That is even worse. Do you wish for the gentleman to think you rude and tell all his acquaintances that you are prideful and vain? No."

Harriett sighed. "You might simply tell me what I should do so I do not continue to disappoint you."

"Very well. You must meet his eyes only briefly, as you have demonstrated well, but then shift your gaze to your nearest acquaintance and begin a conversation. Show that you are more interested in them than in a flirtation across the ballroom."

Harriett nodded. "And what should I do if I meet a gentleman that I *do* wish to engage in a flirtation with across the ballroom?"

A slight smile touched her mother's lips. "Then you most certainly should not glance away immediately. You must hold his gaze and effect the slightest of smiles. You then might lower your gaze bashfully before stealing one more glance at his face. If his gaze holds steadfastly on you the entire time, then you will know that he is interested in you as well. He will likely arrange with the master of ceremonies to receive an introduction. Until then, glance at him every so often, and keep your smiles minimal and proper."

This was the part of her season that Harriett had begun to dread. She had always looked forward to the purchasing of new dresses and accessories, but the part about finding a husband—the most important part of her season—was beginning to bear down on her shoulders with a weight she couldn't explain. She had always dreamed of making an advantageous match, and she had always been certain she could. Practicing here with her mother, however, filled her with sudden uncertainty. She pushed away her doubts. This season was a grand opportunity, and she was very likely to find a suitable husband there. There was nothing to fret over, she assured herself. But then why was her stomach in knots?

One name flitted across her mind in answer: William. *Blast* the man.

"Let us practice again," her mother said.

"Are you a desirable gentleman or an undesirable one?" Harriett asked.

"Desirable this time."

Harriett was preparing her most flirtatious yet miniscule smile, when the butler cleared his throat in the doorway. "There is a Mr. William Harrison waiting in the entry hall."

Chapter 9

Harriett's insides flipped. She exchanged a glance with her mother, who tossed her a suspicious glance. "Invite him in, I suppose."

The butler nodded, widening the door and ushering William forward. Harriett straightened her posture, her heart leaping. She had nearly forgotten that he had wanted to paint with her that day, and she had certainly forgotten to tell her mother about it.

William walked through the doorway, wearing his usual smile. Paired with his green waistcoat, his eyes were striking as they met hers across the room. She instantly forgot the lessons her mother had just given her, and her gaze dropped to the floor. Drat. She tried to correct it by looking to the side, but that only landed her gaze on her mother, who stared at her with immense disapproval.

"Mr. Harrison, what brings you here this morning?" her

mother asked. Even amid the vexation that Harriett suspected to be brewing inside the woman, she managed to maintain a polite tone.

"I thought I might call upon your daughter to join me this afternoon as I make an attempt at painting the view of Brighton from my back property."

Harriett would have a new appreciation for her mother's willpower if she managed to say no to William's cajoling smile.

After throwing a quick glance in Harriett's direction, her mother gave a slight nod. "I suppose that would be all right."

"We will have a respectable chaperone in my sister, Maria, of course."

Harriett's mother seemed to be appeased by that fact. She had always loved Maria Harrison. "Ah. I see. Very well."

"That is, of course, only if Miss Weston still wishes to join me." William met Harriett's eyes, and she felt her own willpower shrinking.

"Yes." She cringed at the strained tone in her voice. "I would be glad to." Harriett didn't know whether she should be relieved or disappointed that his memory had not been restored overnight. How long did these sorts of things last?

As she stared across the room at William, she realized that this outing could be counted as their final meeting, if she included their walk and the dinner party the night before. After today, her wager with her sister would be complete, and she could go back to planning her season, without William Harrison hanging over her every thought and action. Grace would have no argument to make against her about how she never gave him a chance or how 'she would like him if she only made an effort to reacquaint herself with him.' Harriett would finally be able to prove Grace wrong in the entire matter.

"Shall we go?" William flashed her a smile. "I have a set of easels in place on the back property of my family's home and a gig out front to convey us there."

"Yes." Harriett stepped out of the drawing room at William's side, following him to the front door. Maria sat on the back of the gig, smiling and waving as they exited the house.

William smiled down at her as they walked. "I suspect it would not surprise you that my mother has insisted that I return to living with her and the rest of my family until I am well again. I feel perfectly well, but I have decided to appease her. I am not allowed to return to my work as a barrister until I am considered to be 'right in the head.'" He gave a hard laugh. "The lawyers of my acquaintance will not give me any cases."

Harriett watched the frustration in his expression with growing concern. How difficult it would be to forget so much of your life. She felt a strong pang of empathy for him in that moment. "I am sorry this happened to you. I cannot comprehend how frustrating it must be."

"It is not so very bad," he said. "Without work, I am free to spend more time with you." He gave a soft smile, one that seemed to thread straight through her skin and puncture her heart.

She swallowed. His eyes captured her, and she found herself staring into them for so long that she began counting the streaks of light green and dark green, mingled with little flecks of gold. She did not know how to respond. Was he trying to court her? Or was he simply trying to uncover more of his past through the time he spent with her?

"Miss Weston!" Maria called down from the back of the gig. "You look positively lovely this morning. Doesn't she look well, William?"

"Very well."

Harriett didn't look at his face as he handed her up into the gig, stepping in beside her. He took the reins.

Maria heaved a sigh. "I suspect Miss Weston would make a much better subject for your painting today than the same boring sea that you have painted multiple times before." Her voice brightened. "Perhaps you might paint her portrait."

Harriett stiffened. Her face burned. The thought of William studying her closely enough to depict her in a painting set her stomach churning. "Oh, no, the sea is a much more suitable subject."

William set the horse in motion, a pensive expression clouding his features. "No, I do believe Maria is right. You are far more lovely than the sea."

"Yes, that is my point!" Maria said.

William nudged Harriett softly with his elbow, and she lifted her gaze to his face. He wore a wickedly teasing smile, one that she had not seen on his face since they were children. "I promise I will not depict you in resemblance of an elephant."

She laughed, shaking her head. "Even an elephant would be a much more interesting subject. I would love the opportunity to paint or sketch an elephant. Imagine if there were an elephant standing in the center of your back lawn, posing for a portrait. Would that not be spectacular?"

William nodded, his eyes lighting up at the idea. "It would be, but I would still prefer you. After all, an elephant might trample my painting when I finish if it is not satisfactory. He might trample *me* as well."

"Perhaps *I* would trample your painting if it is not satisfactory," Harriett suggested.

"Ah! Is that what you did to earn my mother's disdain?"

She shook her head, effecting a teasing smile of her own. "Not quite. But I did invite an elephant onto your property once. He was mistaken for your grandfather by the poor-sighted artist, and your mother was forced to hang its portrait in the drawing room, or else risk being trampled by the prideful creature. She has resented me for it ever since."

William tipped his head back with a laugh, and Harriett couldn't help but admire the sound. She joined him, laughing until her cheeks ached.

She quickly stopped herself when she realized what she had said. What was she doing? Her imagination had run away with her in a way that it hadn't since she was a child. Even in the short time she had been spending with William, he had already stirred up a change within her. If she intended to be respected and admired in London, she would have no room for foolish imaginings. She needed to become more practical, logical, and refined. Not the opposite.

"I'm sorry," she said. "I should not have said that."

William sighed, his laughter still hanging in his voice. "Not to worry. My mother is not here to scold us for it this time."

Harriett's cheeks burned. She had just made a clear mockery of William's dead grandfather. She couldn't possibly have been more disrespectful. She lowered her voice. "May your grandfather rest in peace."

Maria's laughter still rang through the air behind them. "I thought I was the only one that found his portrait peculiar. I suspect it truly was a poor-sighted artist that depicted him, for none of his descendants have inherited the ears or nose. Each time I pass the portrait I thank my good fortune that I did not."

William laughed. Harriett watched him carefully, her lips twitching. They were not making a mockery of William's grandfather, but only his portrait. She justified the laughter that bubbled up through her chest, bursting out of her mouth in a most unladylike manner.

A few minutes later, they arrived on the back property of William's family's home. Given the elevated state of her imagination, Harriett could easily imagine Mrs. Harrison peering out the back window of the house, her eyes narrowed into slits and her hands pressing into fists against the glass. Harriett had never seen a woman so protective of her adult son.

After helping her down from the gig, William led her to the back lawn, where two easels rested near the gardens. The Harrison's property neighbored the woods on the south side, but the sea was in clear view to the east. As promised, the two easels were set up facing the ocean, a small table set with various paints and brushes between them. Maria walked past them, humming as she went, and found a place beside a nearby tree. She sat down, leaning her back against the trunk, and withdrew a book.

"Please do paint Miss Weston, William," Maria said as she lowered her gaze to the pages. "I would dearly love to see it."

William raised his eyebrows in Harriett's direction. "May I?"

Harriett's stomach flipped all over again. "Only if you allow me to paint a portrait of you."

He chuckled. "Very well." He rubbed his chin. "Is this becoming a competition of sorts? Maria, will you be the judge? Whoever creates a more accurate depiction of the other will be allowed a prize."

Before Maria could answer, Harriett cut in. "What is this prize you speak of?"

"Whatever the winner so desires." He flashed an endearing grin.

"That is quite a broad request."

"Are you afraid of what I might ask?"

"No…" She paused. Was she? She did not trust the grin on his face. He seemed far too excited about the endeavor to be unsure of what he would ask of her. Likely he already knew, and that terrified her. "I only think that this is not a fair competition. You painted that beautiful landscape in your family's drawing room. My painting ability is quite juvenile in comparison."

"I very well could have forgotten how to paint in such a way."

Harriett shook her head. "I don't think a talent like that can be taught or forgotten. You will pick up that paintbrush and create a masterpiece whether you feel able to or not, I am confident."

He tipped his head to the side. "Are you finally admitting that you are a masterpiece?"

Harriett scoffed. "No. I am attempting to offer you a compliment, so please accept it."

He grinned. "But you will not accept mine."

"Is this another competition you are proposing? Of who can most properly accept praise?"

He dropped his head down with a chuckle, picking up his smallest paintbrush. "Please hold still so I may begin."

Harriett gave an exasperated sigh, but the mirthful expression on William's face pulled a smile from her without permission. Maria had fallen silent, lowering her eyes back to her book with a mischievous grin.

As much as Harriett hated to admit it to herself, and she would *never* admit it to Grace, she quite enjoyed William's company. She had forgotten what it was like to laugh with him and talk with him, and even imagine ridiculous scenarios with him. She felt as if she had stepped back in time to the days when she had been carefree and happy and… different. Very different.

What had changed her? Just like William, she had undertaken a great change that last day at the ocean. She had become guarded, careful, and uneasy. It wasn't fair for a girl of twelve to be granted such feelings for a young boy, feelings she did not know what to do with, feelings she was far from understanding. She had reacted wrongly, and William had been left with the consequences. Harriett wished Emily had never come to visit—that she had never encouraged her to be so cruel.

"You have told me about my family." William flashed a smile. "Now tell me about yours." He focused on his canvas before darting his eyes up to her face.

"You met my mother and father yesterday," Harriett said, "and you must thank your father on their behalf when he returns from his hunting trip. He has offered to purchase many of our horses and a portion of our property with which to build his new stables. In doing so, he will be helping my family immensely."

"Now I have proof that my father is both kind and wise." He smiled. "Tell me more."

"Well, I also have a younger sister, Grace. She is married now to the new Lord Coventry, formerly Lord Ramsbury." She studied his face for any recognition of the name, but it was blank. "She is quite happy. They are away visiting some of her husband's family in the north."

"Have I met Grace before?" William asked as he touched his paintbrush to the canvas.

"Yes. She was among us when we played by the ocean as children. You knew Grace well." She could see a storm of questions in William's eyes, hovering close to the surface. Harriett laughed as she remembered their games. "When we pretended to be pirates, she was the ship's carpenter, and I was the quartermaster. You were the captain, of course."

"Was I a fair and just captain? Dashing and handsome?"

"Not so. You were something of a wicked captain. You forced me to walk the plank when I said—" she stopped herself abruptly.

William lowered his paintbrush. "When you said what, exactly?" His lips were smiling, but his green eyes bore into hers, demanding an answer.

"When I said I would rather marry a fish than a pirate captain." She stifled the laughter that bubbled out of her mouth.

"And I was the pirate captain?"

She nodded. She had been lying when she said it, of course, as most young girls would have done to hide their affection for a boy. But she was not about to tell William that.

"I made you walk the plank because you would not marry me in our imaginary game? Did you find a fish to marry instead in the sea after you walked the plank?"

"Yes, I did find a fish. He was quite handsome and agreeable and we have since lived happily ever after."

"What a fortunate fish, indeed." Half his mouth quirked upward as he spoke, as if he were trying to repress a grin. His gaze swept over her face as he painted a stroke on his canvas. Harriett felt her cheeks burn. He continued staring at her for a long moment. "It seems, in forcing you to walk the plank for refusing my hand, I found you every bit as charming then as I do now."

The heat on her face had spread over her forehead, tingling on the tips of her ears. What was wrong with her? William had always easily made her blush.

He chuckled, studying his palette lazily. "It seems I will need to mix a new shade for the pink of your cheeks." He winked at her, picking up the red paint.

She couldn't help but smile. He was teasing her. She found her gaze darting toward the grass. Drat. She had already failed her mother's lesson multiple times over. She searched her mind in an attempt to recall the rules her mother had taught her. When an undesirable gentleman met her eyes, she was supposed to look to the side and engage in conversation with someone new. The problem with this arrangement, however, was that Maria was seated far to her right, and William was on her left, attempting to make a portrait of her. She could not look away even if she wanted to.

More troubling than that, was her realization that deep in her heart, William was not an undesirable gentleman. Not at all. In terms of character, he was everything she had ever wanted. In terms of social standing, family, and possessions, however, he was not. She assured herself that she would find a man in London that had all the requirements of a husband to fit the wishes of her uncle, mother, father, and herself. But when William met her eyes again, her wayward heart skittered.

She held as still as she could for the next several hours, and William continued asking her questions about her family and herself. He rarely spoke of his own life, but when he did, the same frustration entered his eyes. It never lasted more than a few short moments before his smile returned, and she was left to wonder if it had ever left his face. When her neck started to become sore and her back ached from holding her posture, William set down his brushes, gazing down at his canvas.

"Have you finished?" Harriett asked.

"Not yet." He stretched his shoulders. "But I should take you back to your home for dinner. I will have to finish another day. Are you otherwise engaged tomorrow afternoon?"

She hesitated. Today was her third time meeting with William. She was no longer obligated to see him through her wager with Grace. The relief she had expected to feel at this moment was something much closer to disappointment. How could she force him to leave his portrait unfinished? That would be extremely rude of her. Yes. She had to see him one more time—*only* one more time, so he could finish his painting. Her heart pounded with a warning, giving rise to her doubt once again. Did she dare see him a fourth time? The more time she spent with him, the more difficult it would be to walk away. Before she could stop it, her traitorous reply slipped out. "I am not engaged."

William smiled. "Perfect. I will come by your house at the same time tomorrow."

She nodded, wringing her hands together. Why had she agreed to this? "May I see what you have painted thus far?"

He quickly lifted his canvas off the easel, keeping it turned away from her. He threw her a secretive glance. "Certainly not. It is a surprise."

"You *are* painting me as an elephant!" Harriett raised an accusatory finger at him.

He chuckled. "You will find out tomorrow."

She eyed him with enough suspicion to make him laugh.

Tomorrow. That would be the last time she sat with William and talked with him and laughed with him. Grace would be even more appeased when she learned Harriett had extended the wager to four meetings. Harriett took comfort in that thought as William returned her home.

Chapter 10

As promised, William arrived at the same time the next afternoon. Harriett had never thought that sitting still for hours could be entertaining, but with William nearby, she was perfectly content. There were moments when William had to pause his painting because he had begun laughing too heartily, and moments when Harriett lost her prim expression and posture as a result of something William said. She didn't realize until later that those pauses had added time to William's painting process, and he would need to take another afternoon to finish.

"Shall I pick you up at the same time tomorrow?" he asked as they stood and began walking back to the gig.

The hesitation Harriett had felt the day before had grown distant, drowned out by the smile that ached her cheeks. "Yes."

And so the next day, William came again. Maria took

up her usual place beneath a tree, and Harriett sat in her chair as William took up his brushes. After an hour, he declared that they ought to take a break, and brought out a chessboard and a tray of grapes, cheese, and bread. William had forgotten many of the rules of the game, and so Harriett taught him how to play. She won each match, and by the time William surrendered, the sun had begun its descent over the grass where they sat. Maria had fallen asleep beneath the tree, and William declared that he would finish his painting the next afternoon instead.

Harriett's mother had expressed her silent disapproval each time William came calling, reminding her of her upcoming season, but Harriett continued to assure her that she was simply helping William finish his project. Mrs. Harrison's disapproval had been more outright, as Harriett had glimpsed her on more than one occasion, watching from the back window of the house, her brow more stern than even Harriett's imagination had projected it to be.

When the next afternoon came, William took a short thirty minutes to complete the painting, rising to stretch his back with a smile.

"It is nothing extraordinary," he said. "In fact, I think I ought to never paint your portrait ever again." He laughed. "No matter how enjoyable the process was."

Harriett's cheeks grew hot. "Let me see it," she said, coming to her feet, choosing to ignore his last comment. William had discovered every possible way to make her blush over the last several days, and she had discovered no way to stop it from happening.

William took a step back, allowing Harriett to circle around the back of his easel. She gasped, covering her mouth with one hand as she took in the painting. She did not know what she had expected to see, but the result was, contrary to William's claim, extraordinary. He had painted her smiling, with her lips pressed together. Her eyes sparked with joy and imagination, so much so that she found her breath catching in her chest. Is that what she looked like now? Her gaze followed the crisp and soft lines, the pastel colors, and the slight pink he had depicted in her cheeks. The woman in the portrait was beautiful. Is this how William saw her? Her heart thudded against her chest. She didn't know what to say.

"William—this is… you are very talented." She stared up at him in awe.

"Do you like it?"

Her hand flitted to her chest, pressing against her heart. "I love it. I never knew you were such an artist."

He appeared pleased in the most humble way, his eyes dropping away from hers. His mouth curved in a genuine smile. "Nor did I."

"Now it is my turn," Harriett said, walking back to her canvas. "It will likely take me all afternoon, so you ought to make yourself comfortable."

William raised his eyebrows, taking a seat on his stool. He turned fully toward her, clasping his hands in his lap. She began mixing her colors, glancing carefully at his hair, eyes, skin, and lips. She would paint only his shoulders, so she chose a black for his jacket, white for his cravat, and mixed her green paint with white to create the pale shade of his waistcoat.

She began at the top, painting the different shades and highlights of his hair, from the darkest brown to a reddish highlight where the sun reflected, betraying the carrot hue his hair had once been as a child.

Their conversation continued with ease, and Harriett found that she had to set down her brush multiple times, her laughter causing her hand to shake too much to paint. She scolded him each time he made her laugh or blush, yet he continued to do so. A distant feeling continued buzzing in her chest, one she had not felt in its fullest for a long time. As she examined the sensation, warm and bright and all-encompassing, she realized it was happiness. True happiness, the kind that came only from human interaction and friendship. For years she had spent her days scouring the shops of town for a new accessory to make her happy. She had made so many purchases—she had run out of pin money. She had tried and failed to fill the emptiness within her with things that could never fill it. She had felt joy spending time with Grace, but after she married and moved away from home, Harriett had begun to feel more alone than she had ever felt before.

As Harriett watched William's various expressions as he spoke and laughed, she felt something else within her, a spark, a flame, a desire to never be parted from the sound of his laugh or the smile in his voice.

The moment she recognized it, she extinguished it, stamping out the warmth and fire as quickly as she could. Throwing away her caution had been very dangerous. She could not allow herself to travel down the path she had burned long ago. Perhaps if things had been different—if William recalled the events of their past and still cared for her—she might have allowed it. But the moment he remembered, he would shun her like his mother had. He would hate her, and Harriett would be left just as broken as she had left him all those years ago.

The sun was going down by the time she finished the painting, and her hand shook. She hadn't wanted to extend her project into multiple days as William had, so she had rushed through the final details. William came to stand over her shoulder, studying the canvas. She didn't dare look at him.

When his silence persisted for several seconds, she turned her gaze to his face, her curiosity becoming too much. The look on William's face shocked her, the clear admiration in his eyes as he turned them on her. "You are more talented than you claim. Your technique is unlike any I have ever seen. Your colors are much bolder than mine."

"I meant to convey your personality in the portrait," she explained. "You are much bolder than I am. You have always been quite brave, and seem to fear nothing. You have never been one to pass by unnoticed by those around you, but it is not because of your need for attention, but the need everyone else feels to pay attention to you. They cannot help it." She studied the painting as she spoke.

When she glanced at his face again, she found him watching her, a look she couldn't name burning in his eyes. Was it admiration? Longing? She was fairly certain he wasn't longing for her, but rather longing for the memories he had lost. Whatever it might have been, it set her heart skipping.

"Shall we have Maria judge the paintings?" Harriett asked, her voice too quick. She looked over her shoulder, catching William's sister's gaze from her place under the tree. "Maria, come see the portraits!"

William arched one eyebrow, causing a small crease to appear in his forehead. "I thought you didn't wish to make it a competition?"

He was right. She hadn't. But she had needed a distraction, and it was the first thing she had thought of. She cursed herself for her impetuosity. "I changed my mind. I think I have a chance at winning." Truly, she had no chance at all.

Maria came to stand behind Harriett, her dark eyes inquisitive as she looked at the painting Harriett had done of William. "Oh, how lovely. You have captured his expression quite perfectly. Well, his new expression. Before falling from his horse he had become rather serious." Maria imitated the look, drawing her eyebrows together before falling into laughter.

William frowned. "I never wish to effect such a stern expression ever again. Please stop me if I dare appear so severe, even after I remember the reason for it." He eyed Harriett carefully, as if he were beginning to fully suspect her hand in his past severity. Something inside her plummeted at the thought. He was right to be suspicious.

"And this!" Maria stood behind William's easel. "This is marvelous! You must admit that I was right in declaring that Miss Weston would make a much better subject than the boring ocean." She let out a squeal of delight, skipping over to Harriett and grabbing her hands. "I did not think William could properly convey your beauty, but he has succeeded. Although your piece is also quite lovely, I'm afraid I must declare William the winner."

William pumped his fist in the air with a cheer. Harriett scowled.

"I am honored to have won," he said, "even if the competition was not fair. Credit is owed to Miss Weston's beauty, to be sure."

Maria nodded. "Yes, that may have swayed my opinion slightly."

William smiled at Harriett before rubbing his jaw. "Now what shall I request for my prize?"

Harriett's stomach seemed to have filled with lead. She had been dreading this part. She watched his face as he mulled over his decision. Her trepidation grew with each second that passed. Would he ask her to tell him exactly what she had done to hurt him? That was the question she feared the most. She had been foolish spending so many hours in William's company, and even more foolish for reminding him of the competition.

He drew a deep breath before speaking. "I would ask that you give me your painting."

"Is that all?" She almost sighed in relief.

He gave a soft smile. "Yes. It might help me figure out who I truly am, and I would very much like to become those things you described me to be."

Warmth spread though her, stretching all the way out to her hands and feet. "Very well. May I have yours?"

"No."

"No?"

"Absolutely not." William shook his head, taking it off his easel although it wasn't yet dry. "I will keep this one as well."

She placed one hand on her hip. "That is not fair."

"Neither is your beauty." William winked, causing Maria to giggle and Harriett to blush all over again. He walked toward her, a small smile pulling on the corners of his lips. "And it may help me figure you out as well. You are a mystery, Harriett, one that I will take no small amount of pleasure in solving."

Harriett scolded her heart for leaping at his words. "Perchance you never see me again after today?"

William's eyes searched hers, curious, kind, and bright. She could very well become lost in them and never resurface if she was not careful. He drew a deep breath. "Then that would be quite a shame."

Chapter 11

Cool morning wind whipped against William's skin as he rode over the path in the woods—the same path on which he had taken his fall. He took great care this time to slow down as the trees grew thicker around him. He was certain that both his mother and the physician would be dismayed to learn that he had taken a ride that morning, but aside from his lack of memory and a dull ache in the back of his head, he was completely recovered.

He guided his horse to the clearing that Harriett had shown him that first day he had walked with her. Bringing his horse to a halt, he tethered his reins to a nearby tree and stood, arms crossed, examining his surroundings. Perhaps if he could recall the moment just before he struck his head, it would be the start to remembering everything else. He closed his eyes, straining his mind to recall even the smallest detail. The effort left his head pounding, and he opened his eyes with a sigh of frustration.

The physician had met with him again the day before, shortly after he had finished painting portraits with Harriett. Mr. Gibbs had once again assured him that his memory would eventually come back, but William was beginning to have his doubts.

He sat down against the trunk of a nearby tree, scooping up a handful of pebbles from the dirt. He tossed them into the clearing one at a time. He didn't know how long he stayed there, thinking and pondering, but he eventually heard the sound of distant hoofbeats. He stood as the sound grew closer.

A short minute later, he could see a familiar tan horse trotting toward his place in the clearing, with Maria atop the side saddle.

"Mama awoke in terror when she discovered you were not at home," Maria said as her horse came to a halt. "I told her that you were perfectly capable of going on a ride, and that it was highly unlikely that you would ever lose your seat again, but she did not believe me." She laughed, stroking her hand over her horse's mane. "I suspect her behavior may seem very strange to you, but you must know she only acts that way because she loves you very much. It has devastated her to know you do not remember us all."

William couldn't deny that his mother's behavior had been frustrating, but he hadn't stopped to fully consider how his lost memory had affected her. He couldn't help but feel a pang of guilt for having such ill thoughts toward her. Surely she meant well. It must have been very difficult for her to be forgotten by her own child.

He walked over to Maria's horse to help her down. The

moment her feet touched the ground, she skipped away from him. She had more energy than he had ever seen in a woman, at least that he could remember. He had learned that she was seventeen years old, but her face still held the characteristics of a girl much younger, with a petite and slightly upturned nose, round cheeks, and large, expressive eyes.

"She sent me to ensure you were still alive and not unconscious yet again." Maria grinned at him as she crouched down to study an insect that had landed on a leaf on the ground.

"Perhaps if I were to fall unconscious now I would wake up with my memories again."

"Are you certain you want them back?" Maria asked. "You seem much happier without them. How wonderful it would be to forget the dreadful things of life. You do not remember what sorrow feels like."

"My life could not have been so very bad. I had a profession I enjoyed, a family, a home. Surely there are many happy things I have forgotten as well." William gazed up at the leaves, spinning on their stems with the breeze. They had changed color, a myriad of red, orange, and yellow above, with brown, dead leaves on the ground beneath his feet. "But what I am most curious about is Harriett Weston." He turned his gaze to Maria. "Do you know what it is that she isn't telling me? Do you know what happened between us?"

Maria hesitated, walking back to her horse and running her fingers over its muzzle. William was not yet well acquainted with Maria's movements and expressions, but he could tell she was hiding something. "Well," she said, "I know that you were friends as children, and I was always too young to join you in your games. You and Harriett often played much longer than the other children, and were the very dearest of friends. And then, one day, something changed. You returned home and never went back. I don't believe Harriett ever went back either." Maria cast her eyes heavenward. "You kept to your room on most days, and when you left for boarding school and returned, there were few characteristics remaining of the lighthearted boy you had once been. You were always kind, but you had lost your humor and teasing and you took everything much too seriously. Until now, of course."

William already knew the things she said, but still found them difficult to believe. "Is that all you know?"

"I know that you once cared for Harriett very much. I do not know what changed your mind about her. You avoided invitations in which she might be in attendance, even after you had returned from school. But you could not avoid it forever." She shook her head, her curls bouncing beneath her bonnet. "I remember a ball at the assembly rooms two years ago. It was my first ball, and I saw the way you looked at Harriett. It was similar to the way you look at her now, but with less… hope." She shrugged. "It seems you changed your mind about her, but your heart could never be changed, no matter how hard you tried."

William listened in silence, a certain clarity coming to his mind as his sister spoke. From the moment he had first seen Harriett after waking up, he had felt a connection to her. He knew she had played a large role in his life, and he wished he could remember what had happened. She had told him she didn't wish to speak of it, and she, much like Maria, appeared to be hiding something from him.

Maria stepped away from the horse, threading her fingers together in front of her. "Do you remember when I asked you at dinner if you had read the letter I had sent to you on your trip with Papa? Did you ever receive it?"

William vaguely recalled Maria mentioning a letter. "When was it expected to arrive?"

Maria shrugged one shoulder. "I only asked because you came back to Brighton shortly after I sent it to the hunting lodge. The letter was addressed to me with the request that I send it on to you. I suspect Lady Coventry did not know the address of your hunting lodge."

"Lady Coventry?" William's brow furrowed.

"Harriett's younger sister, Grace. The attached note declared the contents of the letter to be of great importance. I was nearly curious enough to open the letter myself, but thought it right to send it to you per Grace's request."

William could see his reflection in Maria's dark eyes as they stared up at him, wide and clear. He was now even more confused. "I have not found such a letter among my possessions. Do you suppose it arrived at the lodge after I had already left?"

Maria seemed to consider the idea. "It is possible. But it also might have been what led you to return early to Brighton. If the contents of the letter were indeed urgent…"

William felt on the brink of a discovery—of what, he was uncertain. But Maria's words throbbed in his ears, pulsing and loud, as if to tell his brain that they were important to remember. "If I did indeed receive the letter and come back to Brighton, I must find it."

Maria frowned. "You said you have not seen it among your possessions."

"Perhaps I left it at the hunting lodge. I might have read it and then left in a hurry." William began pacing over the dead leaves and dirt that covered the forest floor.

"That is a great possibility."

He did not like the idea that he had come back to Brighton on urgent business and then had forgotten what that urgent business was. Anxiety filled him, clutching in his chest like a metal fist. "You must write Grace and inquire about what the letter entailed."

Maria's brow tightened. "But I do not know where to address such a letter. Harriett said she was visiting her husband's relatives on the northern coast. Even if I did discover her location, it could be weeks before we receive her reply."

"Harriett will know where to address it," William said.

"She will likely find it strange that I am asking." Maria bit her lip. "I am not as well acquainted with Grace as I am with Harriett. Grace was always reading when Harriett and I went to the Brighton shops together. Perhaps you may write to Papa and ask if you left a letter behind at the lodge?"

William nodded. That was likely a much better plan, one that would bring him answers more quickly than waiting for a letter to return from northern England. Whatever it was that this letter entailed, he knew it was of great importance. He could feel it in his bones. His excitement faltered, however, when he realized his father would be returning home soon. His letter would not reach him until after his father had already departed the lodge. "He will be gone before a letter reaches him. I must search my house here. I might have missed it."

Maria sighed. "That is true. I do hope you find it. I am quite curious over what that letter contained. It was quite strange."

Quite strange indeed. William felt a surge of energy within him, a spark of hope. The feeling grew, speeding up his pulse and quickening his breath. He knew, without a doubt, that the letter would bring him clarity. He had a strong suspicion that the letter Maria spoke of was the reason he had returned to Brighton. Now he needed only to find it and discover what that reason was.

"We ought to return home soon," Maria said, "lest we have to revive Mama from a fainting with the smelling salts."

William laughed, the sound strained under his racing thoughts. "I will be there shortly. I must stop by my house first and search for the letter. Please tell Mama that I am alive and well, and she need not worry."

Maria shook her head. "Mama will worry no matter what I say to her."

"Then do all you can to placate her until I return."

"I will try." Maria returned to her horse's side, and William moved forward to help her mount. She smiled down at him. "Do tell me if you find the letter. I am at least as curious as you are, perhaps even more so."

He nodded his agreement just as she picked up the reins, setting off toward home. The moment she was out of sight, William mounted his horse and started off toward his house on the other side of the woods.

A few minutes later, he arrived, hurrying through the front doors and crossing the entryway to the stairs. He took them two at a time. When he reached his bedroom door, he went immediately to the wardrobe, searching every pocket and fold of his clothing. His search revealed nothing. After searching the rest of his room, he moved downstairs to the study, rummaging through the stacks of paper on his desk, thumbing through the pages of the books on the shelves.

He eventually sat down at his desk in frustration, rest-ing his head in his hands. What would he do if the letter was never found? He would have to wait until Grace returned to Brighton and ask her personally what the letter entailed.

He stood, stretching his back and wandering out the door. He paced the hallway, struggling to think of any other place the letter might be hiding. As he walked the length of the hall, he stopped at a door, open just a crack. Bright sunlight came through it, and he took hold of the handle as he entered the room. A large window rested on the opposite wall, the drapes pulled open to reveal a view of the nearby sea. Shelves lined the walls, each one covered in painting supplies—brushes, blank canvases, oil paints, water colors, and wooden palettes. He walked slowly forward, stopping at a white sheet, draped over something short and angular. He bent over, picked the sheet up by the corner, and pulled it gently off.

Beneath it, lay a stack of paintings. He drew a breath, sitting down on the ground beside them. He had sent a servant to fetch the supplies when he had painted with Harriett, and hadn't thought to ask where they were located. All at once, the room became familiar. He recognized the window from the place he was sitting. He recognized the painting in front of him. He tried to cling to the wave of memory that had suddenly struck him, but the moment it came, it deserted him again, leaving only a few small and insignificant memories in its wake: the hours he had spent in this room working on his paintings, a whisper of longing, and the color of a stormy sky. He recalled the joy he felt in the exercise of painting, in creating a reflection of something tangible and beautiful.

He touched the corner of the first painting, as if to anchor himself to this new reality and the new emotions that pulsed within him. When had he painted this? What had caused him to feel the things he now felt?

The painting was of a girl, dressed in a lilac colored gown, her back turned, her honey-blonde hair flowing about her shoulders as she faced an unsettled sea. The dark sky settled all around her, a melancholy pervading the image.

Although William could not see her face, it was clear to him who the girl in the painting was.

It was Miss Harriett Weston.

Chapter 12

It had been nearly two weeks since Harriett had received Grace's last letter. She had forgotten to send her a response, what with the significance of the subject Grace had been inquiring after. She had asked Harriett to write her promptly when William returned to Brighton and to tell her every detail of their courtship. The time Harriett had been spending with William, however, was not a courtship, at least not an official one. He had not spoken to her father expressing his intentions to court and marry her. He was simply trying to establish a friendship between them. Yes, that was it. In fact, Harriett was quite certain that all she was to him was a mystery.

And she intended to keep it that way. She had grown far too careless over the last several days.

Sitting down at her desk, she picked up her quill, wet with ink.

Dearest Grace, she wrote.

I am very glad to hear that you are enjoying yourself in the north. I must admit that before you left I wondered if you would find anything to admire in the dreary atmosphere, but I suppose if you have Edward near, there will always be something for you to admire.

Harriett grinned. Grace would appreciate her sentiment. Grace might even suspect that Harriett was becoming one of her own kind: A hopeless romantic.

As I write this, I can very well imagine you skimming over my introductory phrases until your eyes catch on the name 'William Harrison,' at which point you will pause and read each word that follows with intense focus. Now I would guess that you are laughing over the accuracy of my assumption. Well, I'm afraid these words you were so very excited for are going to come as a vast disappointment. Yes, William has returned to Brighton, but we are not courting. I can now imagine the alarm in your expression, but please, do not worry, for I have not forgotten our wager. I have already completed the wager, even going beyond the required three meetings. I will not bore you with the details, for they are of little consequence. I can now prove to you, as I always said I would, that William and I are not the perfect match.

Do not be so upset over this, for I have news that is going to make it all better. Uncle Cornelius has been so very generous and arranged for me to attend the upcoming season in London! Can you believe it? I will have an opportunity to find a man who possesses wealth, a title, and perhaps even a family that I can tolerate (or whom can tolerate me.) So you see, William would never have filled that role. After all, in two short months I will be on my way to London, and will never see him again.

It is my hope that the rest of your trip is delightful, and you do not allow my news about William to affect your happiness in the slightest.

With love,

Harriett

She blew on the ink to dry it. The words she had just written caused an unexpected string of ache to wrap around her, squeezing and pinching. She had been looking forward to her season for her entire life. How had she allowed William to turn her feelings of excitement into feelings of hesitation?

She creased the parchment, her movements firm and angry. Since they had painted portraits, and ever since he had left her side, he had haunted her thoughts. When she was focused, she could avoid thinking of him, but in her avoidance of thinking of him, she was still *indeed* thinking of him. When her mind was absent in the minutes before falling asleep, thoughts of his smile or his laugh or his handsome face entered her mind uninvited, and it often took her a long while to dispel them.

Pressing her head against the oak of her writing desk, she groaned. Why must he be so charming?

She had successfully avoided him for years, but now it seemed she had no way to avoid him. Until she went to London. The string of ache pulled so tight that she felt it might choke her. In desperation, she ruffled through the papers on her desk, withdrawing the list she had made on the day Uncle Cornelius had surprised her with news of her season. She read over the words she had written.

Necessary steps to take in preparation for London:

1. Improve my knowledge of fashion and assist in the creation of the most beautiful gowns I have ever worn, and create hems of such intricacy and embellishment that they put to shame all other hems that have ever brushed the floor of Almack's.
2. Decorate my own bonnets, so that when I am asked where the handsome accessory was made, I may claim it as a work of my own hand, thus adding to my accomplishments in the eye of all potential suitors.

3. Learn a new number on the pianoforte, one that will be begged to be performed at every social assembly.

She took a deep breath. It was time to add a few items of great importance to the list.

4. Banish every thought of William Harrison, no matter how pleasant it may be to dwell upon.

5. Ensure that I am never alone with William.

6. Remain formal in any interaction I may have with William, and make it clear that I do not intend to further my acquaintance with him.

Harriett paused as a surge of guilt turned her stomach over, and she added:

But be sure to do so in a much kinder manner than I did the last time.

She set down her quill, the guilt spreading inside her like a sudden fire, one she no longer knew how to put out. In truth, she had never felt a more keen sense of regret than she did now. She regretted not treating William with the kindness in which he had treated her. She regretted pushing him away. She couldn't help but blame herself for the change she had seen in William over the years. It was the same change she had seen in herself.

In the weeks since he had come to her family's drawing room to thank her for saving his life, she had felt as if he were clipping the strings of a mask from around her face, peeling away layers of falsehood and barriers she had not known were there. He was stoking a fire in her chest, a brightness, a hope that she had not felt for a long time. She felt like he was handing her pieces of herself that she had lost a long time ago.

Shining through it all, however, were her dreams. They had not disappeared, they were not part of the mask. She dreamed of a life that William could not give her. She had grown up in a family of modest income, and had never expected to be given a chance to make her bows in London society. That chance had come to her now, and she could not give it away. Along with that chance came the opportunity to make a match that would give her the life she had always dreamed of, a life in which she could live in great comfort and respect. William worked for a living, he had a small home, and his mother despised Harriett. To allow him closer to her would only bring hurt. It would hurt William, it would hurt his mother, it would hurt Harriett's family—especially her uncle and mother, for they were so excited for her season—and it would hurt Harriett too. The very moment William recalled his old memories and remembered why he had stayed away from her, it would break her heart.

All she could do was continue her plans for London. As she stood from her desk, she tried to bolster her excitement, crossing the room to her wardrobe. She would need to stand out in her attire if she was to be noticed among so many women. She planned to visit the shops that day to purchase embellishments for the bonnet she was currently decorating, and would need to stop by the milliner's shop to seek inspiration in her project. At the thought, a spark of genuine excitement grew in her chest.

Feeling much more like herself, she fetched her jacket and met her mother downstairs to take their trip into town.

"The blue best suits your eyes," Harriett's mother said as she held a satin ribbon up to her daughter's face.

"Both ribbons are blue, Mama. But I do think this one more closely resembles the ocean, and this one the sky." Harriett took the ribbon from her mother's hand, comparing it to the one she currently held. She wished she had brought her bonnet with her. She had already attached a trio of artificial flowers, and she couldn't quite recall the shade of pink on the petals. She wanted to choose the best shade of blue to complement the pink.

"It does not matter so much that the shade of blue goes

well with the pink, my dear. What will matter most is the shade of blue in comparison with your eyes. And so I say again, I think the ocean blue is the only suitable option we have." Her mother had been all patience until that point. Her voice had taken on an exasperated tone.

A new voice came from behind them, deep and familiar. "I'm afraid I must contradict you, Mrs. Weston."

Harriett's breath caught in her chest. *What was William doing here?* She became as rigid as the floorboards beneath her.

"Ah, Mr. Harrison, how do you do? Are you recovering well?" Harriett's mother asked.

Harriett only turned for the sake of propriety, much to the dismay of her frantic heart. She met William's eyes, warm and green, staring down at her with amusement. Maria stood behind him, holding a cap trimmed with red velvet. "I am quite well, thank you, Mrs. Weston," William said. "And you?"

"Quite well, indeed," Harriett's mother replied. "But I do wonder what you meant in your contradiction."

William's lips quirked upward. "The nature of my contradiction is that I do believe Miss Weston would look lovely with any shade of ribbon about her face."

Harriett's mother gave a soft laugh. Only Harriett could hear the underlying concern in it. It seemed William's flirting troubled her mother as much as it troubled her. "Oh, Mr. Harrison, that is very kind of you to say, but I'm afraid we cannot take any risks with a single piece of Harriett's wardrobe."

His brow furrowed slightly. "And why is that?"

"These ribbons are for one of my daughter's headpieces for the upcoming season. She is making her debut in

London and we cannot afford to dress her in anything less than the height of fashion and beauty."

Harriett didn't dare look up at William. She had neglected to tell him of her plans to leave Brighton soon. How would he react? She still did not know if he was trying to court her, but even if she had the slightest suspicion, she should have given him the courtesy of letting him know of her plans to enter the London marriage mart. Her cheeks grew hot at the centers.

"Yes," her mother continued, "we have high hopes for Harriett. I do believe she will be admired far and wide in London. I daresay all her dance cards will be full and she will be called upon daily by titled and wealthy gentlemen."

Had her mother emphasized the words *titled* and *wealthy*? Harriett couldn't be certain. But what she could be certain of was the level of discomfort she currently felt, and the way the feeling intensified when she felt William's gaze on the side of her face.

"I will offer no contradiction on that point," he said. "I have no doubt your daughter will be widely admired."

Harriett glanced up at him. His mouth was smiling, but his jaw clenched as he bowed in their direction. "Maria and I must be going. Good day, Mrs. Weston. Miss Weston."

In a matter of seconds he was gone, Maria trailing behind him. She glanced at Harriett over her shoulder before exiting the shop, a look of curiosity in her large eyes.

Harriett's mother sighed, turning toward her daughter. "I do hope that was enough to deflect Mr. Harrison's advances. He seems to have taken great interest in you since his accident. He is not as quiet and dull as I once thought him to be. He is an amiable young man. I do not wish for him to be greatly heartbroken."

"His attention toward me is strictly a result of my actions toward saving his life. He is grateful, that is all." Harriett's words fell hollow and dull in her own ears. "There is more to it than that," her mother said, her voice grim.

"What do you mean?"

"I do believe he is forming an attachment to you, my dear. You must take every precaution to fend off his attention. Do you remember our lesson on how to divert an undesirable gentleman?"

Harriett nodded. She did not wish to review the steps her mother had tried to engrain in her. She clamped her mouth shut and turned her attention back to the ribbons which hung nearby. Much to her mother's delight, Harriett chose the ocean blue ribbon. After making their purchases, they exited the shop into the increasingly cold autumn air.

Harriett awoke the next morning in a daze. She had dreamt that Uncle Cornelius had changed his mind about sending her to London for the season, choosing instead to send her to London to work as a seamstress, where she would be forced to work her fingers to the bone at all hours of the day and the night. She was the least experienced of all the seamstresses, and therefore was required to sit in the outermost circle, furthest from the single lantern in the center of the room.

Her eyes stung when she opened them to the bright morning light streaming through her window. She groaned, rubbing them as she sat up. The relief of escaping her nightmare was temporary, for she remembered the expression she had seen on William's face the day before in town.

Had she mistaken the disappointment in his eyes? The fact that she had not told him about her season before now had given her yet another thing to regret.

A few minutes later, her maid arrived to help her get ready, and she made her way downstairs to the breakfast room. She loaded her plate at the sidebar, focusing on the delicious scents that wafted up from the fresh eggs, ham, bread, and cheese. Distracted as she was, she didn't notice her mother enter the room until she stood directly behind her, one eyebrow raised in obvious disapproval.

"Good morning, Mama," Harriett said. "What is the matter?" She didn't think she could have done anything wrong yet that day, for she had only just left her room.

"What is the meaning of this?" Her mother extended a neatly wrapped bouquet of lilacs, a string of twine connecting them all. "These came this morning from Mr. Harrison."

Harriett's heart leapt, then picked up speed. This could only mean one thing. William was indeed trying to court her. To make a gesture such as sending flowers and his calling card meant he intended to see her again soon. She was fairly certain her own expression mirrored her mother's, surprise and a bit of dismay. "Mama, you must know I have done nothing to try to encourage him. You saw me in town yesterday. I hardly spoke a word to him."

Her mother nodded, her lips forming a firm line. "Yes, I do not blame you entirely for this. If friendly indifference will not work, then you must resort to being slightly aloof toward him. This is good, actually. It will give you the needed practice for London."

Harriett questioned the wisdom of practicing the art

of diverting a gentleman's attention on William. She couldn't possibly be cruel toward him again. "I'm certain he is simply thanking me for saving his life."

"Oh, Harriett. I'm afraid not. He is smitten with you, and we must put an end to it."

Harriett found swallowing increasingly difficult as she stared down at the beautiful flowers that William had sent to her. Was he truly smitten with her? The very idea made her feel as if her feet were floating off the ground.

Her mother sighed. "I cannot imagine why he would make an attempt to court you when he knows you are soon to depart for London. When he comes calling today, you may go with him—to refuse would be utterly rude—but you must ensure that your intentions are made known. Be straightforward, but not to the point of rudeness."

Harriett nodded, her mind spinning. Her mother was right in wondering why William would try to court her. He knew Harriett was leaving soon, that she would in all likelihood find a match in London. There must have been a different motivation for his actions. His curiosity toward her was born from more than attraction. He knew that she had played a part in his past, and he was trying to figure out what it was. Harriett couldn't find the words to explain it all to her mother, so she simply continued nodding like a ninny.

After today, she could forget about William Harrison once and for all. She swallowed. How many times had she told herself that before? How many times has she tried and failed to forget him? The number was becoming too great to count.

Chapter 13

William set off for Weston Manor around two o'clock, taking the shortcut through the woods as he always did. He had chosen to take Harriett on a ride through Brighton in his family's finest phaeton. The excursion would give him plenty of time to talk with her, to try to riddle out the truth of his past as well as the feelings for her that grew steadily within his heart.

These feelings were not new. He sensed that he had cared for Harriett much longer than the two weeks since he had become reacquainted with her. He knew she had made an impact—an irrevocable one—on his heart and his mind. Whether it was good or bad, he didn't yet know. What he did know was that her mother's words in town the day before had struck him deeply with envy and disappointment. The thought of Harriett in London, being pursued by men of rank and title, irked him more than he cared to admit.

When he arrived at her home, he knocked thrice on the door. The butler let him inside and to the drawing room, where Harriett and her mother sat waiting. The light that filtered through the windows met Harriett's hair, bringing forward the palest hues, sharpening the blue of her intelligent eyes. He couldn't read her expression as he stepped forward, greeting both women in turn.

"Miss Weston, I wondered if you would join me for a ride this afternoon?" he asked.

Something in Mrs. Weston's expression appeared vexed. Her eyebrows arched slightly and her mouth pinched as she stared at him. It seemed both his mother and Mrs. Weston found little to admire in the other's children.

Harriett glanced at her mother, then looked down at the ground, a small smile on her lips. Had she experienced the same thought he had? Her smile faded as quickly as it had come, replaced with a look of deep contemplation. "I suppose so."

She supposed? William had not been hoping for such a deflated response. He studied her distant expression as she left her mother's side and came to join him. He extended his arm to her as they exited the house and made their way to the phaeton. She stopped in front of it, glancing up at him expectantly.

He didn't move.

"I—I do not think I can get up without assistance." Her voice came out quiet. When he made no move to assist her, she raised both eyebrows. "Are you going to help me up?"

He shrugged. "I suppose so."

She seemed to catch onto his teasing, for her cheeks darkened a shade as he extended his hand to her. She took it reluctantly, her lips twitching as if to prevent herself from smiling. Why was she suddenly acting so reserved?

He stepped up into the phaeton, taking a seat beside her. "Are you still angry with me for taking your painting?" he asked.

She glanced at him from the corner of her eye. "Yes, if you must know, I am still quite angry over that."

He laughed, sensing the teasing in her voice. He set the horses in motion, the large wheels of the phaeton creaking as they began revolving. "If it truly means so much to you, then I will return it. You may hang it on your wall and stare at it every time you find yourself missing me."

A true smile bloomed on her cheeks, and she shook her head. "That will not be necessary. You have not been absent for long enough for me to miss you. I have seen you much more often these last two weeks than I ever did before." She had turned her head to fully face him now. It seemed now that they were moving away from her home and her mother's influence, she was acting like herself once again.

"Yes, but you will be away soon, when you leave for London." He gave a soft smile, even though the words ached inside him. "Will you miss me then?"

She was silent for a long moment before turning away from him, her poke bonnet hiding most of her face from view. When she finally spoke, her voice was barely louder than a whisper. "Why are you doing this?"

"Doing what?"

One of her eyes emerged from behind her bonnet, tentative, shy. "Are you trying to... court me? I will be leaving for London very soon, as you know, and there is only one reason a young woman goes to London for the season."

He gripped the reins as they turned a corner. They headed down the wooded path once again. He intended to take her toward the path that bordered the sea, circle the royal pavilion and come back around through the woods. He threw her a half smile. "And what might that reason be?"

"You know perfectly well. Do not pretend otherwise."

"I'm afraid I do not."

She cast him a skeptical look that made him laugh. He did indeed remember why young women went to London, but he wanted to hear her say it. If it earned him one of her endearing blushes, all the better.

She let out a long sigh, and hesitated again, as if she were embarrassed to say it. He watched with growing amusement as she struggled for the words. "To find a husband, of course."

The uncertainty in her voice beckoned him onward. "Have you ever considered that you might be able to find a husband elsewhere?"

She cast him a look of chagrin. "William! This is an entirely inappropriate conversation to be having."

"Yes, but you just called me William. Is that not also entirely inappropriate?"

She pressed her lips together, a look he had come to realize produced a deep dimple in her right cheek. "Forgive me, but you were behaving like you did as a child, so the name slipped right out."

He sat back, looking straight ahead, in part to steer accurately, and in part to distract himself from her charming dimple. He put on a teasing smile. "I wonder if *I* might go to London to find a wife."

"I think it would be wise for you to regain your memory before seeking a wife."

"Of course, that was my plan. I would never be foolish enough to seek a wife without being in my right mind. I would likely choose the wrong sort of woman." He felt Harriett's gaze on the side of his face. He met her eyes.

"So... you are not trying to court me?" Her brow was furrowed, her bright blue eyes inquisitive.

He considered the question, still unsure of the answer. There was so much about Harriett that he didn't yet know or understand. She intrigued him. Not only that, but he found her beautiful and charming, and he had yet to find anyone whose company he enjoyed more. As he examined the feelings in his heart, he found a great deal of mystery, much like the mystery that surrounded the woman beside him. What would happen when he once again recalled his past—if he ever did? Would he still like her? Or would he share his mother's opinion? He couldn't imagine not liking her. In fact, he suspected he was falling in love with her.

It was more than a suspicion. He knew it.

He shrugged, knowing it would likely irk her to no end. "What do you think?"

"Are you asking whether I think we are courting or not?"

William nodded, laughing at the shock in her features.

"I don't think so," she said. "I think you are spending time with me to discover this mystery that you think I'm hiding." After a pause, she added, "What do *you* think?"

He chuckled. "It would not be fair to tell you."

"Why not?"

"Because I deserve to be a bit mysterious too."

She narrowed her eyes at him as they passed under a large tree, the shade blocking them from the warmth of the afternoon sun. The autumn air crawled over his skin, making him shiver. He urged his horses forward.

"I am not intentionally mysterious," she said.

"Yet you are intentionally hiding the truth of our past interactions." William watched as she glanced down at her lap, her features unsettled like the loose, fallen leaves on the path. They passed the thick patch of trees, coming to a clearing that was bathed in warm sunlight. The leaves appeared brighter here, the warm colors intensified by the brightness all around them. William stopped the phaeton, guiding his horses to a slow halt.

"What are you doing?" Harriett asked.

"Enjoying the sunshine." He tipped his head back. "As soon as winter comes there will be no more of it. I ought to enjoy it while I still can." As he said the words, he thought of Harriett, and how very soon, things between them would change. Either she would go to London, or he would regain his memory. Or both. It terrified him. He had come to enjoy this life free of the cares of his past. He wasn't sure he wanted to remember why he had avoided Harriett for so many years. He pushed away his melancholy thoughts. He would enjoy Harriett's company while he could. If he lost her, then at least he would still have these memories to hold onto.

She laughed, tipping her face up to the sun. "I cannot believe I am doing this." Her voice was giddy, breathless. "But it feels so wonderful."

William watched the delight on her face as she soaked in the sunrays.

"I feel very much like Grace," she said. "My sister has never been careful about her complexion getting too much sunlight, but I have been vigilant. I never leave the house without my bonnet and rarely without a parasol."

The angle in which her head was tipped allowed the sunlight to touch her cheeks, away from the shade of her current headwear. He admired the sweep of her lashes against her cheeks as she closed her eyes, the dimple near her mouth, and the width of her smile. In combination with her laughter, it made his heart skip. Without thinking, he sat closer.

"It seems I have been a terrible influence on you," he said.

She laughed harder, her eyes still closed. "Oh, William. You have always been a terrible influence."

He shook his head, though she couldn't see it. "I think it must have been you that was the terrible influence."

"Not at all," she said in a resolute voice.

He laughed, lifting his hand to brush away a curl that had fallen over the side of her face.

Her eyes shot open, meeting his. He still held his fingers against her cheek, tracing the curve of her face. He stared into her eyes, at the mixture of fear and longing within them. A blush began to creep over her skin, and it took all his concentration not to gather her into his arms and kiss her. As he watched her eyes lower to his mouth, he had the fleeting thought that perhaps she would not object to the idea. He glanced at her rosy lips. His heart raced. "I do not believe that for one moment," he said.

With Herculean strength, he lowered his hand, pulling his gaze away from her enchanting lips. He picked up the reins, setting the horses in motion once again. Awkward silence fell between them as the large wheels of the phaeton rotated over the path. To kiss her would have been acutely unwise.

"I hope your mother will not blame me for any freckles

you might have procured this afternoon," William said, hoping to dispel the discomfort in the air.

The tenseness between them evaporated as Harriett laughed. "Why not? If everything must be fair, then my mother should come to hate you as much as yours hates me. A freckle to blemish my face just before my season will be reason enough for you to gain her eternal dislike."

"Hmm." He rubbed his jaw. "But then she will never allow me to court you."

"It is my father's permission you must seek," she said. Her eyes widened. "I am not suggesting that you *should* seek his permission, I simply mean to say that if you ever did intend to court me, then you would first need to acquire it."

He nodded slowly, throwing her a teasing grin. "I understand the prerequisites to courtship and marriage."

"I assumed you didn't remember since you claimed not to know why young women travel to London for the season."

He laughed. "You have caught me in a lie."

"Are there others?" she asked with an exaggerated gasp. "Have you only been pretending to not remember me all this time?"

He taunted her with his silence, staring straight ahead as they followed the path out of the trees.

"William!" A note of genuine concern had entered her voice.

He burst into laughter. "I told you I must remain mysterious."

She sighed. "Please stop being mysterious. I do not like it."

"Only if you stop too." He raised one eyebrow, challenging her with his gaze. Did he dare ask her about the mysterious letter that her sister had sent him? She might have known something about it.

Harriett gazed past him at the ocean, her forehead creased with worry, deep thought evident in her eyes. "Have *any* of your memories returned?"

"It is difficult to explain. I have not regained memories as much as I have regained emotions. When I look at something, I remember how I once felt about it. I realized this when I was in my house looking at my old paintings and the view from the window." He followed her gaze briefly to the ocean before returning his attention to his horses once again. He found a place for them to stop and helped Harriett down onto the path. He extended his arm, and they began walking toward the sea. The tiny pebbles of the sand crunched underfoot as they walked, the sound mingled with the gently crashing waves and the brief passages of conversation from the occasional passersby.

"For example," he said, "when I look at the ocean, I feel many things. I feel lonely, but I also feel happiness, freedom, and belonging. I don't fully understand what these emotions mean, but I'm certain they were born of memories that I am still missing." The path sloped downhill, and they walked closer to the sea. "When I look at my childhood home, I feel a mixture of contentedness, unease, and a sense of being trapped. When I look at my paintings, I feel a sense of release, peace, and comfort."

He stopped walking when they reached the base of the path. He turned his face toward her, tipping his head down to look into her eyes. "And when I look at you..." He paused, drawing a deep breath. He tried to decipher the abundance of emotions that came to the surface. Of all the people, places, and things he had seen since waking up, it was Harriett that brought the greatest onslaught of emotions. When he finally spoke, his voice came out hoarse. "I feel the relief, the joy, and the overwhelming astonishment that comes when one has found something that they have spent agonizing years searching for."

Harriett stared up at him, her eyes turning liquid, pooling with unshed tears. She blinked fast, turning her gaze away from him. Had he said something wrong? She seemed to compose herself, a small smile touching her lips as she shook her head. "You have not been searching for me."

"How do you know that?" he asked. "Perhaps you did not want to be found."

"Perhaps."

He stared down at her for a long moment before a gust of sudden wind distracted them both, the waves of the sea growing larger.

The vast majority of tourists that had come to Brighton had left at the end of the summer, but there were some, come to experience the rumored healing power of the waters, that would remain in town until the sea became too cold to submerge themselves in. The small number of tourists that were out on the beach today wrapped their cloaks and jackets tighter, glancing up at the sky as the sun became hidden behind a cloud.

Harriett shivered as she stared out at the bobbing waves. "I will miss you when I go to London, William. You have become a very dear friend."

When he had first seen her in her drawing room, he had teased her about not being called her friend. He had wanted to be her friend. But now, the word *friend* felt like an insignificant and inadequate description for what had grown between them. The connection he felt to her was far more important than a simple friendship. He swallowed the disappointment that rose in his chest. "As have you."

She smiled up at him, but there was something in her eyes that reflected the way he felt. Distant, disappointed, and reluctantly resigned.

"As friends, though, I do believe we ought not to keep secrets from one another," William said.

Harriett raised one eyebrow. "Will you never give up?"

He smiled. "Never."

She exhaled, long and slow. The wind whipped at the curls that fell around her face, and he wished he could brush them away again. No, he would never give up. He would never give up trying to discover the truth of his past, he would never give up reclaiming his work as a barrister, and he would never give up on Harriett. He wanted her by his side for as long as he could. As long as there was hope, even the slightest bit, he would continue trying to change her mind about leaving. Determination grew within him, powerful and bright, banishing the cloudy darkness that surrounded them.

Her expression had become increasingly troubled, her brows drawing together as they always did when he brought up her secrets.

He couldn't help but smile. "You do not need to tell me anything, Harriett. It does not matter what happened in the past. I do not care."

Her eyes rounded in surprise. "You cannot say that you don't care if you don't remember what I said."

"I hope I never remember. But if I do, then I will be shocked if it does anything to change what I feel for you now." He stepped closer to her, unable to resist the wayward curl any longer. He caught it between his fingers, tucking it behind her ear.

A light mist of tears clouded her eyes and she looked down. "You hated me."

"I can think of something stronger than hate." William's heart pounded. Did he love her? He didn't dare use the word now. It would only scare her away, but as he examined his heart, he realized that he did. He was in love with Harriett.

"What is it?" she asked, her voice quiet, filled with anticipation.

"Friendship." He took her hand, squeezing it tightly in his before raising it to his lips, hoping to convey that she was his dearest friend, but she meant more, much more to him than just that. When he lowered her hand, he didn't let go.

"Do *you* still mean to keep secrets from me?" Harriett asked.

"You may ask me anything you wish." He had never felt more courageous than he did in that moment, surrounded by wind and dark clouds and an agitated sea, holding Harriett's hand.

She drew a deep breath, as if she were afraid to ask her question. "Are you trying to court me?"

"You already asked me that," William said with a chuckle.

"You did not answer. You only attempted to be more mysterious than me." Her lips twisted into a smirk.

He sighed. "Yes, Harriett, I am trying to court you."

Her eyes widened again, her hand pulling slightly against his grasp before relaxing. He wrapped her hand up in both of his, smiling in an effort to calm her expression.

"Why?" she asked, her voice breathless. "You never tried to court me before."

"Because if I do not do it now, I'm afraid I never will.

I'm not certain I want to be the man my family tells me I was before my accident. That man was a coward, weak, too afraid to pursue what he wanted. And I'm fairly certain I have always wanted you, Harriett." Silence thrummed between them. He had just said it. He wanted her, he loved her, and now she knew. He felt his own cheeks burning when she didn't respond, the uncertainty in her expression clearly displayed. He released her hand, hoping to lighten the tension that had fallen between them.

"I should take you home," William said. "It looks like it may rain soon."

She nodded quickly, avoiding contact with his gaze as they walked back to the phaeton and he helped her up. The ride back to Weston manor took an excruciatingly long time, and William tried to turn the conversation to lighter topics, such as the weather, but there were only so many interesting things one could say about the weather.

Harriett attempted to turn the conversation to her family, and William was once again tempted to ask about the letter her sister had sent him, but he refrained. He would learn soon enough. His father would be back within days.

When he walked her up to the front doors of the house, she hardly looked at him. After stammering a quick 'thank you,' she entered the house. Rain began falling in heavy droplets so that the moment he stepped away from the shelter of the porch, he became soaked. The open top of his phaeton would give him no shelter on his ride home. He tried to keep a positive attitude. Yes, he would be soaked. Yes, Harriett seemed to want nothing to do with him. But he had seen something in her downcast eyes as she walked away that given him enough reason to keep hope alive inside him.

Chapter 14

Harriett had learned to hide her anxiety in the presence of Uncle Cornelius. He was far too perceptive to miss it if she showed even the slightest sign. Her London preparations were well underway. She and her mother had taken countless trips back and forth from the milliner's, cordwainer's, and modiste's, gathering all the various accessories that she would need to make her grand London debut. She had also been enduring lesson after lesson from her mother about proper societal behavior, and she had been, in her mother's words, performing quite well.

The more Harriett thought about her life in the last three weeks since her ride with William, she realized that it was the most performing she had ever done. She had been acting. She was acting as if she did not care at all for

William. She was acting as if she were excited to go to London, as if she were happy.

It had been her mother's idea to turn William away each time he came calling. She had claimed that her daughter was not feeling well, and sent him on his way. Harriett could not help but wonder if William's memories had returned, or if his injuries had at least healed. She missed him. With her wager complete, she needed to exercise self-discipline. Seeing William could only inflict harm. He could very well keep her in Brighton, wasting her uncle's investment and dampening her mother's happiness.

Luckily Harriett's London preparations had given her much in the way of distraction, however it was not strong enough. William still slipped into her idle thoughts when she was unprepared, stinging her with a fresh wave of grief and longing. She hadn't thought she could ever miss him so much. As much as it ached her to separate herself from him once again, she knew it was for the best. Her uncle had already invested so much in her, in this season. She had never seen her parents so happy either, so pleased with her. She did not wish to disappoint them.

Even if she did find the courage to stay and see William again, she knew that it was not fair to continue deceiving him. He would eventually remember why they were not meant to be together. He would remember why he had avoided her all those years, and he would begin doing so again. She would have missed her opportunity to go to London, chasing after a boy that could never love her in return. She couldn't imagine the heartbreak that would come if he married her, ignorant of their past, and then, when his memories returned, he grew to hate her. She couldn't bear the thought of being hated by her husband. She dreamt of being loved, cherished, and living in a comfortable and grand home. That was what she wanted and needed. Even if she told William what had happened between them, it wouldn't be enough.

Feelings were much stronger than words.

"My dear Harriett, what is troubling you?" Uncle Cornelius's cheerful voice had taken on a tone of concern as he stared across the tea table at her.

Drat. She had allowed her emotions to slip into her expression. "Nothing at all. I am quite well."

He raised one thick gray eyebrow. His piercing blue eyes missed nothing behind his spectacles. "Would you lie to your uncle?"

"No." Even that was a lie. She bit her lower lip.

He studied her for a long moment. She picked up her teacup, grateful for the shield it placed between her and her uncle. Her mother sat on the other side of her, oblivious to the anxiety that had just apparently been very clear upon her daughter's face. "Harriett, do tell Cornelius about our last lesson. I am very proud of the results."

Grateful for a distraction, Harriett nodded. "Mama taught me how to ensure that I receive plenty of invitations and calling cards. She also taught me how to fill my dance card at every single ball."

Uncle Cornelius's eyes lit up with glee. "Truly? My, I would be quite happy to hear that you succeed in such an endeavor."

"As will I," Harriett's mother said, her smile nearly as wide as Uncle Cornelius's. "The first step is always to look as beautiful as possible, and to never leave your bedchamber without first dressing to the height of fashion. We selected a number of hair arrangements that will suit her thick blonde hair perfectly. We will show society that dark hair is no longer all the rage. I do believe Harriett could change everyone's perception with just one look." Her face beamed with pride.

Harriett couldn't remember the last time she had seen her mother so happy. She and her husband were finally on their way out of their financial struggle and their daughter was on her way to making a grand debut in London. Even when Grace married an earl she hadn't appeared so pleased as she did now, planning Harriett's season. It was something she had always wished to give her daughters but had never been able to. It seemed her mother was more excited to go to London as a chaperone than Harriett was as a debutante.

"There is no question. Harriett is a rare beauty." Uncle Cornelius winked at her. "I have high hopes for this season, my dear. You are going to fall in love, I am certain."

Harriett's heart stirred with doubt. She pushed it away. If she didn't fall in love in London, that was no matter. She had never been the silly romantic that her sister was, at least not since Emily came to visit nine years before. Harriett could still remember her cousin Emily's large blue eyes as they stared down into hers, sharp and insistent—inarguable. She tried to bite down the memory, but it came anyway.

"Harriett, I find it my duty as your eldest cousin to coach you in what it is to be a proper young lady."

Harriett had just walked through the back door of the house when she found her cousin Emily standing by the window. Harriett blinked twice to take in the young woman's flawless complexion, beautifully curved figure, and large eyes. She had never met this particular cousin before, but Harriett had heard that Emily had been eager to visit Brighton, and Harriett's parents had invited her to stay for a month during the summer. Emily had just arrived that day, and looked far too pretty to have just traveled over a hundred miles. Harriett's mother had told her that Emily was sixteen, though Harriett would not have been surprised if she were older, given the bright, mature beauty of her face.

Harriett wasn't certain of what she should make of her cousin's unsolicited advice, but she nodded politely. "I would be glad to be your pupil."

Emily laughed. Harriett listened intently to the high, soft sound. Is that what a proper lady's laugh was meant to sound like? It was far from her own laugh. "I am pleased to hear that," Emily said, "for there is much work you can do in the coming years to prepare to make a good match and secure a comfortable living. Such things are more important for a woman to secure than anything else." She bent down to be closer to Harriett's height. "What do you suppose makes a 'good' match?"

Harriett puzzled over the question. She did not wish to disappoint her teacher. "A man that is well-suited to the woman, I suppose. One she can make intelligent conversation with, one that she can laugh with, and one that she loves very much."

Emily covered her lips with three gloved fingers, as if to suppress her amusement. "Those things are ideal, and are welcome companions to the most important thing you must look for in a husband, but those things you listed are not by any means necessary. In fact, they may even hinder your ability to find that one *thing that truly matters."*

Harriett scowled. "What is the one thing?"

Emily grinned as if she were sharing a carefully guarded secret. "He must be capable of elevating both you and your family in society. That is all that truly matters. The sooner you learn that, the better."

"Elevating?" Harriett did not quite understand her meaning.

"Yes. There are several ways he can elevate you and your family. First and foremost, you must seek a man that has wealth and property. This will always gain him the most respect in society. If ever possible, try to snare a man who is a titled peer. Never, ever, settle for a man that lacks either of these qualities. You will be a disappointment to everyone in association with you." She straightened her posture and extended her arm. *"Shall we take a walk? I have much more to teach you."*

Harriett smiled up at Emily. How fortunate she was to have such a wise young woman to guide her in the right direction. Harriett could feel the beginnings of a dream within her, a picture of herself managing a beautiful house, wearing beautiful gowns, and feeling very much like a princess. Her mother and father would be so very proud of her.

"How do I secure such a man?" Harriett asked as they walked. She was only twelve years old, but Emily made it clear that it was never too early to begin learning and preparing.

"The first asset that you must have, though not all women are so blessed as you and I, is beauty. I can see that you will grow to be a very handsome woman indeed. You must also become accomplished." She raised one finger. *"Never, ever, ever prioritize anything above the time you must spend practicing your accomplishments. Learn as many languages as you can, learn to play the pianoforte flawlessly, learn painting, singing, and anything you can do that might catch the attention of a gentleman. There is no time for other activities such as playing imaginary games by the ocean."*

Harriett's eyes shot up to Emily, who gave her a knowing glance. *"Your mother told me how you currently enjoy spend-*

ing your days. Twelve is much too old to be doing such things."

Harriett looked down at the grass ahead, her cheeks burning with shame. She had never thought she was too old for such things. William still played with them, and he was fourteen. "Very well. I—I will try to stop."

Emily continued with her teaching for nearly an hour, and Harriett found herself wishing she had brought a pencil and paper with which to record all the wisdom Emily was so generously giving her. When their lesson was finished, Harriett's mother allowed Emily and Harriett to take a trip into town, where they entered nearly every shop, examining all the fine ribbons, jewelry, shawls, hats, shoes, and gowns.

"What do you think of these gloves?" Emily asked.

Harriett felt a surge of pride that such a wise and beautiful woman as Emily would care about her opinion. She stood taller, examining the crocheted gloves carefully. "I think they would suit you quite well."

Emily beamed as she tried them on her dainty hands. After making her purchase, they exited the shop. Across the road, William stood outside the bakery with his older brother Percival. Harriett's smile grew, and she waved, catching his eye. William smiled, motioning for his brother to follow him as they approached.

"William, this is my cousin, Emily. Er—Miss Frampton." Harriett glanced up at Emily, who stared down at William with a hint of disdain. The expression shocked Harriett, and she stared at William with a critical eye. What had Emily found in him to dislike? Harriett could think of nothing she did not like about William, although his teasing was sometimes tiresome, he was a very kind, amiable boy.

"A pleasure to meet you, Miss Frampton." William gave a nod of his head. He was respectful and polite as well, Harriett added to the list of William's positive qualities. What then had Emily found to dislike?

William grinned. "Harriett, I have been trying to convince Percival to join us at the beach for games tomorrow, but he refuses. Will Grace and Rose be there? We cannot leave the pirate ship unattended for an entire day."

Emily's disapproving gaze sharpened.

Harriett hesitated over her words, swallowing hard. "I—well, I do not think I will be there either. I have made plans with my cousin, you see."

"Ah. Very well. I suppose I will conquer the sea beast on my own."

Harriett knew what he was doing. She could tell by the mischievous gleam in his green eyes. He was trying to tempt her to come. It would not work.

"I hope you do, so we may stop playing such ridiculous games." Harriett held her chin high the way Emily did, and gave a quick nod in William's direction. She tried to ignore the confusion on his brow as they turned around. She held tight to Emily's arm as they walked down the path toward home.

"Was that your friend?" Emily asked.

"Yes."

"Is he the son of a gentleman?"

"Yes, they live quite comfortably off their land."

Emily took several steps in silence. "Was that his older brother with him?"

"Yes."

"Hmm. So he will likely inherit nothing."

Harriett had never thought about William's future profession or his living situation. She had never found a reason to worry over such a thing. Why did Emily care so much? "Yes, I suppose Percival will have the property."

"I'm afraid he fancies you," she said. "I had many boys fancy me as a young girl, and I could always tell by the way they teased me and smiled far too much."

"William fancies me? I am like his sister." Harriett scoffed, but her heart started beating faster. She remembered the day he had taught her to ride a horse. She had suspected that he might like her, but she had refused to believe it entirely. She couldn't admit to Emily that she fancied William. Her heart seemed to twirl with excitement. Could it be true? Did William fancy her too?

"My dear, you must make it clear to him as soon as possible that his feelings for you are in vain. You are both very young, his heart will recover. It is better to do so now rather than when you are older and of marriageable age. He could never elevate you in society in his position."

"I would never marry William," Harriett said, her own voice hesitant. "He knows that. We are simply friends."

"Friendship is often the first step to love, and love must never, ever interfere with ambition."

Harriett stared up at Emily, her words piercing through her rebellious heart. She did not want to believe what she was hearing. But Emily, talented, beautiful, successful, accomplished Emily, was much older and much wiser than Harriett. Perhaps she was right.

In that moment, a firm determination grew inside Harriett. She would no longer play ridiculous games with William and her friends. She would learn to be the sort of lady that Emily was, and one day make a match as prestigious as her cousin expected. Nothing could stand in her way.

"You must tell him soon," Emily reaffirmed with raised eyebrows.

Harriett's stomach twisted with fear. How did one go

about such a conversation? She couldn't actually do it. But for her cousin's sake, she nodded.

"I suppose you could go to the beach tomorrow, one last time, and tell him then. After that, you must come back to the house and begin studying and practicing in earnest. Oh, I am so excited to be your teacher in these matters. My older sister was such a help to me in my younger years. Considering that you do not have an older sister, the duty falls to me. It will give me a purpose besides relaxation while I am here in Brighton."

Harriett felt important, like she had suddenly been given a purpose much greater than silly childhood games. She was growing up, and one day soon, she would be just like Emily.

Harriett was pulled out of her memories by her mother's voice, slightly deeper and gentler than Emily's. "I agree with Cornelius, there is certainly something troubling you."

"There is not!" Harriett snapped. She hadn't meant to be so abrupt, but her legs had begun to shake, and her recent thoughts had sent her anxiety surging. She took a deep breath, laughing in an attempt to soften her outburst. "I am simply a bit overwhelmed with all the preparations for London. I do not wish to disappoint either of you."

Her mother seemed to understand, a look of compassion unfolding over her features. "Oh, Harriett, you will not disappoint me. I am already so proud. Picturing you in London has given me something to look forward to these weeks. I know you have been working very hard to prepare."

Uncle Cornelius took a biscuit from the tea tray, taking a small bite before nodding in affirmation. "I cannot imagine myself ever being disappointed in you. There is a reason I have invested in your season. I trust that you will make the entire family so very proud. Above all though, there is nothing I wish for more than your happiness. I hope you know that."

Harriett glanced up at his smiling eyes. Uncle Cornelius found so much joy in the prospect of her season. If she failed him, she could never forgive herself. She couldn't imagine being the source of sadness to a man who had already experienced so much sadness in his life. His beloved wife had died just a few years before. How could Harriett do anything to hinder the joy he found in her trip to London?

"I know," Harriett said. She hadn't expected the tears that sprung to her eyes. "And I believe I will be quite happy in London."

"And even more happy with the exemplary man you are bound to catch." Uncle Cornelius winked, and her mother laughed.

Harriett smiled, ignoring the sickness in the pit of her stomach. The moment she stepped into the shimmering candlelight of a London ballroom, she would recover. Her heart would forget William as it once had. She repeated Emily's lessons in her mind as she sat with her mother and uncle. She tried to feed off of their excitement, but the effort was exhausting and futile.

Chapter 15

William wished his mind would stop producing questions that he had no answers for, and start producing his old memories instead. His mind had been extremely uncooperative of late, and so had his vain efforts to see Harriett again.

Had he misunderstood her expression the day of their ride? He had called upon her twice in the last three weeks, but her mother had turned him away, claiming she was ill. He would have been concerned, but he had seen her from a distance in town a few days before with her mother, appearing perfectly well. He had intended to approach her, but his own mother had been in his company, and the moment the Westons came into view, she had steered him and Maria in the opposite direction.

He stared into the flames in the fireplace in front of him. With a sigh, he turned his attention back to the book of law that he had been studying. He had begun to recall almost everything about his profession, yet he was still not allowed to work. The lawyers that oversaw his actions insisted that he pass a test that required him to recall the details of his last three cases. As of now, he could remember nothing. His father had returned from his hunting trip, and while William liked his father immensely, he was all the more frustrated to learn that his father had no knowledge of the letter Maria had spoken of. As far as William's father knew, William had declared that he had important business to attend to in Brighton just before taking his leave of the lodge.

Frustration had mounted in William's chest, burning in his limbs. As hard as he tried to find them, as much as he wanted them, the answers to his questions refused to come. They would come in their own due time apparently, if they ever did, and he had no power to control the speed of their arrival. The patience it required was more than he currently had.

He placed his hand on his forehead, closing his eyes briefly. He took off his cravat, feeling a rush of heat from the fire and his own anger creeping up his neck.

The sound of movement caught his attention, the rustling of skirts. He opened his eyes, turning to see his mother entering the library. She sat down in a chair beside him, placing her hand lovingly on his arm. "What is the matter?"

He rubbed one side of his face. "Nothing."

"Tell me what is wrong. Perhaps I may be able to help."

William shook his head. "Unless you have the power to bring back my memories, then I do not think you can help me. Or unless you can convince Miss Weston not to go to London."

His mother's brow furrowed and she tightened her grip on his arm. "Why do you care if she goes to London?"

He clenched his jaw, preparing himself for the disapproval that was sure to follow his words. "I love her."

His mother gave a quiet gasp. "No, you do not."

"I do."

"Well, you certainly *should* not." Her upper lip curled with distaste. "That woman is wicked and cruel. She broke your heart and nearly killed you. My young, sweet boy."

William froze. He had heard nothing about the second part of her statement. "Nearly killed me?"

His mother sat up, pulling her hand away from his arm. "I had hoped you would remember these dreadful things on your own." She sighed. "But if you have not remembered by now, I fear you never will. Harriett was foolish enough to swim out in the sea during a storm, and you tried to save her. You nearly drowned because of her and your ridiculous games. Yes, you once loved her. You loved her enough to save her, but did she show any gratitude? No. I do not know exactly what she said to you, for you refused to tell me. But I know that it hurt you. It changed you." She shook her head. "You may think you love her, but I hate her. I suspect you will too once you remember those things."

William's mind raced. Is this what Harriett had been hiding all this time? He had seen no malice in her, no intentional cruelty. He had only seen guilt and regret. Even if his mother's words were true, he was certain Harriett had changed since then. So had he.

"She saved my life too," he said, his voice hard. "Whatever debt she owed in your mind has been repaid. You have no reason to hate her."

"Well I do." His mother's eyes had taken on a fire that

burned hotter than the flames in the hearth. "You deserve much better than Harriett Weston. The very moment you are well again, I am going to introduce you to the daughter of my dearest friend, Lady Bringhurst. You will see that there are much more agreeable women in the world than Miss Weston."

William glared at the floor, his mind and pulse racing. "You are wrong."

"*I* am wrong? You are the one that is not in your right mind, William. I am trying to protect you."

He wasn't even certain if he could believe his mother's words about Harriett. There was only one person who could affirm them, and it was Harriett herself. He stood, crossing the room to the door.

"Where are you going?" His mother asked, her dark eyes flashing.

"To see if Harriett is well." He didn't wait for his mother's response as he left the library and made his way to the stables. Mounting his white stallion, he set off toward Weston Manor.

Harriett had been relieved when, after a few minutes more in the drawing room, her mother and Uncle Cornelius had departed for his home. Her mother was helping with new decorations for her brother's parlor, and so Harriett was left alone.

She tried to think of every possible way she could tell them that she did not want to go to London, but there was no way she could do it that wouldn't hurt them both. She eventually moved to her bedchamber where she sat at her desk and added trim to one of the bonnets she was bringing to London. But just looking at the headpiece sickened her, and she tossed it to the ground.

A swarm of emotions filled her chest. Why had she been in the woods the day William was injured? Why could it not have been someone else that saved his life, someone else that he had been compelled to thank in their drawing room when he awoke?

Her thoughts traveled to Emily's visit once again. The worst of it had come the next day. Alone in her bedchamber, Harriett leaned back against her chair, her resolve too weak to ignore the memory that most haunted her, the events she had been running from for so many years—the things she had done and said to lose William's respect, friendship, and trust forever.

Harriett's legs shook as she walked down the front steps of her house. Emily stood behind her with an encouraging smile. "It must be done eventually. There is no sense in delaying it."

Harriett took comfort in her cousin's confidence. This would be her last time meeting her friends by the ocean to play. It was the last time she would be teased by William, for Emily had said that his teasing was the most clear sign of his affection for her and must be stopped.

Harriett squared her shoulders, effecting the posture that she had seen in her older cousin, walking along the path in the direction of the beach. She had taken the walk so many times, she recognized each and every cobblestone.

The day was dark, with large gray clouds shutting out the sun overhead. The sea appeared more gray than blue as well, more menacing and large as it reflected the ominous black of the sky. Harriett could certainly imagine a sea creature twisting and writhing beneath the surface, but she was not allowed to think such ridiculous things any longer. She shunned her thoughts and focused instead on the matter at hand.

When she reached their spot on the beach, she was surprised to find William there alone. Rose was never late. She knew Grace was at home with a riveting book, but she had fully expected to see Rose there. The fact that it was just William, his back turned to her as he tossed pebbles into the sea, set her heart racing.

As if he sensed her arrival, he turned around, a wide grin pulling on his lips. Under the darkened sky, his hair appeared darker too, and Harriett couldn't help but wonder if it might look like that when he was all grown up.

"Harriett!" He waved, and the wind blew at his hair, tossing it over his forehead. "You have arrived just in time." He tossed the pebbles to the ground and walked toward her. "Since Percival refused to join us, I told him that a wicked witch would seek her revenge for his refusal. He didn't believe me, of course, and called our games ridiculous, so I thought you might help me exact our own revenge on him." He grinned. "We might begin by filling his shoes with sand."

Harriett stopped herself from smiling. Teasing Percival was always an entertaining task, but she remembered her purpose in going to the beach that day. She lifted her chin. "I called our games ridiculous yesterday, don't you remember? Does that mean you plan to send a witch after me as well?"

William tipped his head to the side. "I did wonder why you said that. Was it because your cousin was nearby? She looked to be the sort of person to disapprove of a bit of fun." He laughed, scooping up a handful of sand. "We must hurry, though, because Percival will be returning soon." He started walking away.

"I do not want to."

He whirled around, his brow furrowed. "I thought you would."

She shook her head. "No, it is a very childish thing to do, William."

"You are a child," he said with a laugh. "So am I for a bit longer."

"That does not mean we have to behave with such immaturity."

He eyed her carefully, and Harriett's cheeks burned under his intense study. She still did not know how she was going to bring up the subject Emily had sent her here to breach. It felt entirely unnecessary, but Emily had affirmed that it was of the utmost importance that she get William's sights off of her at once.

"Very well," he said. "We can stay here today if you wish to be so grown up. You like to draw, don't you? Perhaps you might sit quietly and draw a picture. Is that not what grown up ladies do?"

His voice was full of teasing again, and Harriett did not like it one bit. "No, William, I do not wish to stay at all. I came here to tell you something."

He raised both eyebrows. "What do you wish to tell me?"

Her heart pounded and squeezed. What if Emily was wrong? What if William did not fancy her at all? She couldn't possibly say something that would imply that she assumed he wished to marry her one day. They were still children, after all. Certainly a boy of fourteen who quite enjoyed being a child was not thinking so far into the future. The more Harriett pondered over it, the more she found reason to doubt in Emily's words. She quickly stopped herself. No, Emily was right. She had to be right.

But still, Harriett's indecision over her words had left a

gap of silence much too long to be normal. She looked out at the sea and blurted, "I—I wondered if you knew how to swim?" She tried to appear natural, but she cursed herself internally. Where had such a strange question come from? She had panicked.

He smiled. "I don't, actually. That is one thing my mother has never allowed me to do. She thinks the sea is far too dangerous to practice in. She thinks a shark will come eat me or that I'll drown."

Harriett laughed before she could stop herself. Mrs. Harrison had always been very protective of her children. She never allowed Maria to come to the beach with them, and she often watched William from the window of her house, sending her eldest son Percival to stop William if he ever came too close to the ocean. It all seemed to be a bit excessive, but William tried to think of it in a positive light, saying that at least he had a mother that cared for him.

"Do you know how to swim?" William asked.

In truth, Harriett had never tried it. The sea was too large and mysterious, and she was too small. There was no reason for it. Harriett couldn't picture a proper lady swimming around in the ocean. "No, I do not."

William turned his gaze to the sea, a mischievous smile pulling on his lips. "It cannot be so very difficult. My mother is at a neighbor's house for tea this afternoon."

Harriett scowled. "You cannot be suggesting that you are going to try it."

"I am. Are you too afraid? Do you truly believe there is a monster beneath the surface?"

Her frown deepened. Why could he not understand that she no longer believed in such nonsense? Hot anger pulsed in her legs as she walked closer to the water. "Of course I don't."

"Are you certain?" he teased.

"I already told you!" She marched toward the bobbing waves, sudden emotion burning in her throat. She wasn't afraid of the ocean. She wasn't afraid of an imaginary sea creature. She was most afraid of letting go of the things she loved most. She loved playing at the ocean with her friends, and she especially loved the time she spent with William. Today it had to all disappear, whether she wanted it to or not. It was the rebellious child within her that wanted to keep it, but for the sake of her future happiness, she was convinced that it was time to let it go. Why could William not understand that?

With tears clouding her vision, she took the first step into the sea, not even bothering to remove her boots. The hem of her skirt quickly grew heavy with the water, but she continued her steps forward. All she had to do was wade out until the water reached her shoulders, kick her arms and legs a bit, and walk back.

"Harriett," William's voice held a warning, but she didn't listen. "I was only teasing."

Of course he was. He was always teasing her, and she had had enough. She trudged through the water. It chilled her skin, creeping higher up her legs and then her back.

"Harriett, stop." She heard a splash behind her. William had stepped into the water, moving quickly toward her.

"No. I am proving that I am not afraid."

"I believe you," he said in an exasperated voice. He reached out and grabbed her elbow, but she jerked it away, diving forward into the water. She had intended to keep her head above the surface, but she had misjudged the depth of the water. Cold liquid surrounded her head and face, and she kicked her feet desperately, searching for the ocean floor. She could no longer reach it. She pushed her arms downward, gasping for air as her head broke the surface. She blinked the *water from her eyes, surprised and terrified to see how far she had drifted from the shore. Her heart picked up speed, her legs seizing in panic. She could no longer see William. A large wave traveled toward her, and her head submerged again.*

Her lungs felt as if two hot bricks had been placed over them, burning with the lack of air. She struggled to reach the surface, but she did not know how far away it was. She kicked her arms and legs frantically, but her boots and skirts felt as if they weighed tons. Eventually, her head grew light, and her aching arms and legs grew too heavy to move.

Blackness darker than the surrounding water overtook her.

She awoke to the sound of sobs, a choppy, broken sound. Was she crying? It did not sound like herself. Everything echoed, and her chest still burned. She coughed, her eyes gaining the strength to open as water spurted out from her lungs. The rough pebbles of the shore poked against her back and head, and she looked straight up.

It was William, his eyes round and red and filled with tears. "Harriett?" He held her wrists, more tears dripping down his freckled cheeks. "I thought you were dead." His voice was weak, choppy, the same sound as those sobs she had heard. His hair and clothes were soaked.

She sat up, cold and disoriented. The tears on his face troubled her even more than the fact that she had just nearly drowned. He pulled her into his arms, his cheek pressing against hers, and she knew the warm water on his face came from more tears as he held her. His body shook. "Never do that again. Never. What is wrong with you?"

Harriett could not think about what was wrong with her, but only about what was wrong with William. She had never seen him appear so weak, so caring, so afraid. "Did you save me?"

He pulled back, a spark of anger in his eyes. "Yes, you bufflehead. Of course I did. Why did you do that?"

"I thought you couldn't swim."

"I thought I couldn't either. I nearly drowned too."

Harriett's stomach had begun to feel sick. She swallowed hard against her burning throat. "Why did you do that?"

"Why did I do that?" *He blinked, wiping the last of his tears away.* "I couldn't let you die."

"Why not?" *She felt the threat of tears in her own throat.*

He shook his head. "Do you think I would just stand here and watch you drown?"

"Do you care about me, William?" *Harriett could hardly hear her own words as she spoke. Her mind felt as if it were filled with seawater.*

"Of course I do." *His voice grew quiet, shy, and he looked away from her eyes.* "I have always cared for you." *Color began to seep over his cheeks, and Harriett's heart plummeted.*

"Well you shouldn't, William, you really shouldn't. Because one day I am going to marry a duke or an earl or a viscount and I am going to live in a grand house and elevate my family, and you are going to inherit nothing, and be a poor sailor or something of the sort, and I could never, ever, ever, marry you. It is best you know that now, and that you never, ever try to change my mind. Not now, not when I am fourteen like you, and especially not when we are both old enough to marry." *Tears burned behind her eyes at the crease that had formed between William's eyebrows, at the color that had fully flooded his face and the hurt in his eyes. But she couldn't stop now.* "I am never playing with you again. You may continue wasting your time playing foolish, ridiculous, childish games, but I cannot do so any longer. I am not the foolish one, William, you are. I wish never to see you again."

The moment she finished speaking, her breath caught and regret flooded her. William had sat back on his heels, hurt flashing in his eyes. Harriett found the strength to stand up, her heavy skirts trailing behind her as she stumbled over the beach toward her house. Tears streamed down her cheeks and she clutched her burning throat. What had she done? How had she been so cruel to William? Is that what Emily had wanted? She hadn't expected she would feel so terrible. She ran through the back door of the house and up to her room before anyone could see her wet and crying. She slammed the door behind her.

She wanted to apologize to William, but didn't know how. Were there any words that could undo the ones she had already spoken? She didn't think it was possible. As she stared at her reflection, her face wet and red and puffy, and her eyes hard and cold, she realized what Emily hadn't.

It wasn't William who didn't deserve Harriett. It was quite the opposite.

Chapter 16

Harriett wrapped her arms around herself, blinking back the tears that had risen with her memory. After that day she had gone to William's home, more afraid than she had ever been, intending to apologize. But his mother had forbidden it. She had found out what happened, and had sent Harriett away without seeing William.

The days had blended into weeks, the weeks to months, and the months to years after that day by the ocean. Harriett stayed at home, practicing the pianoforte, learning, drawing, and shopping in town. William went off to school. Harriett remembered the first time she saw him after he returned from university, his hair darker, his eyes deep set, his jaw firm. He wasn't a boy any longer. Too much time had passed for her to apologize, or for them to ever be friends again. She have given up, and so had he.

They didn't speak. They hadn't spoken until the day he came to her drawing room to thank her for saving his life. She had never thanked him for saving hers. But he didn't remember. He didn't know how cruel she truly was.

A knock sounded on her door.

"Yes?"

Rebecca opened the door just a crack. "You've a visitor in the drawing room."

"Who is it?"

"Mr. William Harrison. With yer mother away I thought you might like to see him. I caught Mr. Radcliffe in the entry before he could turn Mr. Harrison away."

Harriett's heart leapt with rebellion. She wanted to see William at least one more time before she left, if only to puzzle out her feelings toward him and find the closure she needed. Would it be so very bad? She chewed her lower lip as she regarded Rebecca, whose eyes had taken on a mischievous gleam that could challenge even Grace's.

"Thank you, Rebecca." Harriett stood, the action bringing her shaking legs to attention. She ignored Rebecca's pursed lips and dancing eyes as she walked past her and down the stairs. What if his memory had returned? What if he remembered the terrible things she had said to him?

When she entered the drawing room, however, he was smiling. The moment she saw him standing there, she regretted ever leaving her room. She did not deserve the smile he gave her, the look in his eyes that suggested he had missed her as much as she had missed him over the last three weeks. Her heart pounded.

For a moment he simply stared at her. "Are you in good health?" he asked. "I have been told that you were ill." William's eyes reflected genuine concern.

"I am quite well, thank you. Is your... head... feeling better?" She cringed at the awkwardness of her question.

His lips shifted upward on one side, a crooked smile that set her stomach fluttering. "It still aches every now and again, and my memories are as elusive as ever."

"I hope you recover them very soon." Harriett wrung her hands together. As terrifying as it was to imagine William recollecting his past, it was even more terrifying to imagine if he never did. She stood on the opposite side of the drawing room as far from him as possible. There were at least ten paces between them. Why had he come? Had it truly just been to inquire after her health?

"Are you leaving for London soon?" he asked.

"Yes, we leave at the start of January." As she said it, the reality crashed down upon her. That was a month away.

"I assume you have been quite busy preparing."

"Very busy, yes."

William gave a hard nod. His posture had stiffened. In the silence, he met her eyes for a long moment, evidence of a battle within them. She wished she could tell him that she didn't want to go to London anymore—that she would much rather stay in Brighton with him, but the effects of her recent reflections of the day at the beach haunted her. As she watched him from across the room, she began to notice the signs of unrest in his expression. His smile had fallen, and he ran his hand over his hair with a deep exhale. "Harriett," he sighed, walking forward with large strides.

Her heart jumped as he walked toward her, stopping just inches away. He tipped his head down close, his green eyes insistent as they stared into hers. "Why have you avoided me these past weeks?"

She could hardly breathe with him standing so close.

She could smell the faint scent of soap and fresh parchment on his clothes, feel the warmth radiating from him. His eyes would not let her escape either his proximity or his question. "Venture a guess, William." She sighed. "I am going to London, as you know."

"I do not understand how that is a reason to avoid seeing your friend."

The tips of her ears burned with sudden anger. No, he didn't understand why she couldn't see him. He didn't understand how difficult it had been for her to spend hours planning a season that she no longer wanted. He didn't understand how difficult it was to want *him*, when she could never have him, when she knew that deep inside his injured mind, he despised her as much as his mother did.

"You are not just my friend, William, and you know that." She glared at the ground, but he nudged his knuckle under her chin, lifting her gaze back to his. Her traitorous heart leapt.

"Then why do you push me away?" His eyes pled with her for answers that she couldn't give.

"I do not want to." Her voice came out weak as he traced her cheek with his fingers, his touch burning against her skin.

"Then don't."

"You do not understand, William," she said, exasperated, pulling away from his touch.

He crossed his arms. "Tell me, please. Tell me everything that I do not understand."

Her anger flared. "You do not understand why I must stay away from you!" Emotion choked her, despair and anger, a mixture of cold and heat. Her words spilled out before she could stop them. "I spent years trying to abandon the little girl I once was. I found joy in my dream of the day I could go to London. I finally have my chance." She took a step closer, glaring up at him. "But then *you* took away my dream."

William's brows drew together. "I took your dream?"

"Yes," she sighed in frustration, tears burning behind her eyes. "Because you are much better than new ballgowns and accessories and all the social invitations and praise I could ever receive. You have stepped back into my life as if you had never left, as if I had never forced you out of it, as if—as if you had never stopped caring about me."

"Are you speaking of the day on the beach when you nearly drowned?"

She whirled toward him. "You remember?" she choked.

He took a step closer, crossing his own arms as he stared down at her. She had never seen him so serious, so frustrated. "No, I do not remember anything, but my mother told me."

Tears fell down Harriett's cheeks, and she turned away, facing the door.

"She said I nearly died saving your life." William's voice was gentle. "Is that true?"

Harriett nodded, but she didn't look at him. She couldn't.

"My mother told me that she forbade me from seeing you after that. I'm certain I would have if I had been allowed."

"It wasn't just your mother that hated me, William. You saved my life and all I did was say the most unkind things to you." She took a deep breath, wiping her nose.

He touched her shoulder. "I have said before that I do not care, and I mean it." He sighed in frustration. "Please turn around."

She faced him but couldn't look at his eyes. "Do you want to know what I said to you?"

"I do not care what you said—"

"You cannot say that, William! You cannot say that until you know." The guilt she had been harboring for so long sprung to the surface, choking her with sobs.

William's eyebrows drew together with concern.

She took a deep breath. "There was once a time that we were friends, the very best of friends," Harriett said. "You taught me how to be anything I wanted, just by using my imagination. More than anything else in the world, I wanted to be a princess. That was impossible outside of my imaginings, of course, so I decided that I wanted to be wealthy and beautiful and live in a grand home, where I could wear the most regal gowns and attend social events in London and be the most admired in attendance. My cousin Emily told me that those things were only possible for a girl like me, if I were to marry into such a life. And so that became my ultimate goal. My sole ambition. I learned that I needed to grow up, to stop imagining ridiculous things. When I realized that I would never go to London because my family could not afford it, I thought my opportunity was gone. When my uncle presented me with a chance, I had to take it. I have to go, William."

She sniffed, wiping at her tear-streaked face. "I told you I said things I regret. The day you pulled me from the water, you told me you cared for me, and then I told you that I would never, ever care for someone like you. I told you I could never, ever, love you or marry you, because you did not fit the life that I wanted, the life that Emily taught me to want. You had never looked so hurt or broken, William. I'm sorry. I'm so sorry. You cannot pretend that you do not care, because I know you did. And I cannot bear the thought of you hating me once you remember."

She tried to turn around again, but William stepped forward, taking her wrists in his hands, keeping her from turning away. "None of that matters anymore. If I have learned anything from losing my memories, it's how little the past matters. I don't need it to determine whether I'm happy or lonely or angry or if I love you or not. Consider my mother—her past opinion of you is stopping her from realizing how wonderful you have become. Your past mistakes are keeping you from being happy today. Today is what matters, and today, I'm choosing not to give up on you, Harriett. I cannot excuse the behavior of the man I was before, being too weak to chase after you. All I can do is stand here today and try to explain how much you mean to me." His eyes sparked with that same frustration as before, but it was mingled with admiration, longing, and the same fire that burned within Harriett's chest.

She clung to his words, wanting so badly to believe them.

"If London will make you happy, then go," he said. "You deserve to be happy." His voice lowered, his eyes piercing hers. "But if there is any chance that I can make you happy, then I would be honored to do all I can to ensure you are happy for the rest of your days."

Harriett had never felt more tempted by an offer in her entire life. She could be happy with William, but how long would it last? There had been a reason for his aloofness before, and the moment he remembered it, what would happen? And it was not only her own happiness that she needed to consider. It was the happiness of her mother and uncle as well.

As if the thought had summoned her, Harriett's mother stepped into the drawing room without warning, her gaze sweeping over the scene with alarm. "Mr. Harrison!"

Harriett quickly stepped away from him, her cheeks

blazing. Her mother had seen them standing very close, without another soul in the room to make their meeting appropriate. Harriett wiped at the tears on her cheeks. Her mother composed herself with a deep breath. "Mr. Harrison, if you will please take your leave, I must have a word with my daughter."

William nodded, his eyes meeting Harriett's one more time before he brushed past her and left the room. The moment the door closed, Harriett sat down on the nearby sofa, placing her head in her hands. She had a lecture coming her way, to be sure. She sniffed, filling the silence as her mother's steely gaze surely beat down upon her.

She waited, counting to five in her mind. Nothing. She glanced up, surprised to see that her mother didn't appear angry, but sympathetic. She sat down beside Harriett, the silence deafening as she placed her hand on Harriett's knee. "I always suspected you loved William."

Harriett swallowed, her heart beating fast in confirmation. "How?"

Her mother patted her leg. "It was as obvious as anything could be. You forced yourself to grow up far too fast, and you put ambition before the desires of your heart. Do not suppose that I missed the glances you stole in his direction at every ball and party. I still thought you cared more for a season and a chance at a prestigious match, but I see now how very wrong I was." Guilt played out in the creases on her forehead. "I should not have tried to keep you away from him. I just—I wanted to see you thrive in London. I wanted to go myself." She gave a small smile. "But I would much rather see you happy."

There it was again, the word *happy*. Harriett could scarcely believe the change her mother was exhibiting. "Uncle Cornelius has invested so much in me." She wiped her nose with the handkerchief her mother handed her. "I cannot disappoint him."

"I have been selfish, Harriett. Cornelius is never as selfish as I am. He will understand completely. I should have seen sooner that you no longer wished to go to London."

"It isn't that I do not wish to go… it is just that…" She struggled for words.

"You would rather be here with William."

Harriett nodded, a flood of relief crashing over her as she finally admitted it. "Yes."

Her mother pulled her into a hug, smoothing her hand over her back in large, comforting circles. "Not to worry. I will inform Cornelius of your wishes tomorrow morning, and then in the afternoon I will accompany you to the Harrison's residence so you may deliver the news to William, and I may personally thank Mr. and Mrs. Harrison for the generosity of their investment in our land and horses. Your father might accompany us as well, to express his approval of the match."

Harriett took a deep breath and smiled. "Thank you, Mama." She felt she had been relieved of more burdens that day than she could count. Was it truly possible that William could love her? While a small part of her still doubted the persistence of his current feelings, she pushed her doubts aside. For the first time in weeks, everything felt right around her, as if it had just fallen into its proper place.

Her mother held her even tighter. "Grace will be even more pleased with this than I am."

Harriett laughed. "She will indeed."

Chapter 17

Sleep had come with difficulty the night before, for all Harriett had wanted to do was see William again and tell him that her decision had been made. Her stomach fluttered at the thought of seeing him that afternoon, and a wide smile had refused to leave her cheeks from the moment her eyes opened.

She climbed out of bed with renewed energy, and Rebecca came to help her get ready. She learned that her mother had left before she awoke, off to speak with Uncle Cornelius about Harriett's change of plans. When Rebecca finished her hair, she practically skipped down the stairs, feeling very much like her younger sister, romantic and happy and full of unquenchable excitement. At the thought of Grace, she felt a twinge of bitterness. Grace had been correct all along in assuming that William was the perfect match for Harriett. She had just been too stubborn and afraid to believe it.

Harriett brushed around the banister, making her way to the library. If she was going to act so much like Grace, then she might as well find a book to read too, for Grace had been trying to convince her of the advantages of reading for her entire life. She needed something to pass the time until her mother returned and they took their walk to the Harrisons. Her stomach lurched with nervousness at the thought.

Rebecca had only been away for a few short minutes before she came knocking on the library door. "You've a visitor in the drawing room, miss. Mrs. Harrison, by the looks of her stern brow."

Harriett stood, her own brow tightening as she set down her book. "Are you certain she asked for me?"

"Certain as can be, miss."

What reason could Mrs. Harrison have to pay her a visit? She rubbed her sweating palms against her skirts as she followed Rebecca down the stairs. Apprehension flooded her senses as she took one step closer to the drawing room, and then another. She paused beside a decorative table in the hallway, her heart thudding. She scolded herself for being so afraid. She had no reason to fear Mrs. Harrison. With a deep breath, Harriett stepped inside, trying to maintain a friendly expression.

Mrs. Harrison sat on the settee nearest the pianoforte. Dressed in a dark blue gown covered with a matching robe, she blended in with the dark brocade fabric of the furniture. Her brow was indeed stern, her sharp eyes staring at Harriett as if she were a pest that had wriggled its way into her home, where she was not welcome or wanted. "Good morning, Miss Weston."

Harriett had to remind herself that this was her home, not Mrs. Harrison's, so commanding was the woman's presence on the settee. A knot of dread formed in Harriett's stomach. What could she want? "Good afternoon, Mrs. Harrison." Harriett walked forward, taking a seat across from her. "Would you like some tea? I will ring for it if you wish."

"No, I am well enough, thank you." Mrs. Harrison's voice was deep and gruff. "I will keep my visit short."

Harriett was relieved to hear that, but the presence of William's mother in the drawing room still filled her with unease. "What is the nature of your visit?"

"I have come to discuss your association with my son, William." Mrs. Harrison lifted her chin.

Harriett froze. "Oh."

"You and I both know that William is not currently in his right mind. It has come to my attention that he has been making an attempt to court you, and that you have been quite welcoming of his attention."

Harriett swallowed, trying to sort carefully through the words in her head. "I have not seen William for the last three weeks. Unfortunately I have been too busy with my preparations for London."

"Did you not see him yesterday? He returned home quite out of sorts."

"Well—er—yes, but that is all."

Mrs. Harrison sat more upright, her brows falling flat in a glare. "You have broken his heart a second time and I will not stand for it."

Harriett almost told her that she planned to visit him that day and tell him how much she cared for him, but she had a persistent feeling that Mrs. Harrison would not like to hear that. "Would you rather I court him?"

"No, certainly not. I would rather you leave for London and find a different man, and leave my William in peace. You have nearly been the cause of his death."

Harriett's heart squeezed. She knew the moment Mrs. Harrison spoke of.

"Twice now you have caused him great pain and injury."

"Twice?" Harriett was now even more confused.

Mrs. Harrison sat back, her expression smoothing over. "That is no matter. The daughter of my dearest friend, Lady Bringhurst, a very respectable young lady, is who I wish for William to marry. She is much more deserving of my son. I have come to ask, in the most clear terms possible, if you will promise me that you will stay away from my son indefinitely."

Harriett met the woman's hard gaze, her own heart rebelling against the request. How dare Mrs. Harrison come and ask such a thing of her, even when she knew it would be against her son's wishes? Harriett still worried that William wouldn't love her once he remembered what she said and did, but she could not allow that possibility to control her forever.

She held her chin high, despite the fear that pulsed within her. "I am sorry, but I cannot make such a promise."

Mrs. Harrison showed little emotion, but drew a deep breath. It was chilling the way her brow became smooth and the angry fire fled from her eyes. "Very well. You leave me with no choice. I hoped not to present an ultimatum."

Harriett's skin grew cold. "What do you mean?"

"An *ultimatum*. It means I will set clear terms and consequences to your refusal of my request."

Harriett sat, rigid and silent, waiting for Mrs. Harrison's gruff, unfeeling voice to speak again.

"If I hear that you have been in association with my son, I will ensure that my husband does not do any business with your family. We will not purchase that worthless land, we will not buy those inadequate race horses, and we will not save you from your financial woes. Your parents rely on this investment, and without it, they may be forced to sell this very house. I daresay it will put you all in financial ruin." Her lips turned slightly upward, a show of triumph.

Harriett maintained Mrs. Harrison's gaze, but her stomach roiled. How dare she make such threats against Harriett's family? Her heart thudded with dread, each pulse sending fractures into her composure. Any hope she had begun to have about staying in Brighton, the possibility of continuing her courtship with William, were now shattered, laying in jagged pieces at Mrs. Harrison's feet. There was nothing she could do with her family's reputation and well being in Mrs. Harrison's control. She couldn't refuse a single one of her requests. Mrs. Harrison had Harriett right where she wanted her. Squashed and helpless, like a pest underfoot.

"And you will tell no one of this conversation," Mrs. Harrison said, her voice hard. "If you do, I will just as quickly retract our purchases."

Harriett swallowed the heartbreak that had begun to consume her. "Have you considered that keeping me away from your son may make him unhappy? Have you considered any person's happiness but your own?"

"I am his mother." Her eyes flashed. "I will *always* know best what makes him happy. I saw what you did you him. I saw how much you hurt him. I saw how dangerous you were to him, and how much he grew to dislike you."

Harriett stood, emotion clawing at her throat. "Very

well. I will never see William again. Now please, take your leave. I would be just as pleased never to see you again."

Mrs. Harrison gave a regal nod before standing, sweeping her dark skirts behind her, and exiting the drawing room door. The moment she was gone, Harriett fell back into her chair. She covered her mouth with one hand, her mind racing.

Hopelessness stronger than stone crashed against her heart. Mrs. Harrison had just taken away the choice that had been so clear to her the night before. Now she had no option but to go to London. She would do it for her parents. She would make them proud and ensure their financial security. Her heart ached when she realized she would never see William again. What if she returned from London unattached? How could she live in Brighton and know that she could never marry William, never even be near him? What if he married the daughter of Lady Bringhurst, and she was forced to attend social events with them? The thought sickened her.

She remained in her chair in the drawing room, lacking the strength to move. She repressed her tears, unwilling to shed a single one at the hand of Mrs. Harrison. Cruel, wicked woman! Harriett could not tell her mother, or her father, or Uncle Cornelius, or anyone she trusted. She could not even tell William.

Her mother returned shortly after Mrs. Harrison's departure. Harriett sat up, moving to the pianoforte so it appeared as if she had been practicing. She could not appear ruffled in the slightest.

"Harriett! Oh, you will be so pleased to hear that Cornelius took the news quite well. He holds no bitterness toward you at all. In fact, he is quite overjoyed at the prospect of you marrying William." Her mother came into the room like a flower, bright and carefree, her yellow skirts adding great contrast to the storm that churned in the sky out the window.

"I have changed my mind, Mama," Harriett said. She stared at the black and white keys of the pianoforte.

"Pardon me?"

She glanced up, forcing a smile onto her cheeks. "I have decided I would rather go to London. I'm sorry you wasted a trip to Uncle Cornelius this morning. I will tell him myself that I would still like to go."

Her mother frowned.

"In fact, I have been practicing my music so I will be prepared to perform at every available opportunity." Her words came out quick, strangled by the emotion in her throat.

"Harriett—"

"I am going! Nothing can keep me here, Mama. I am very excited, I truly am. I was being foolish last night, for I was very tired and was not thinking clearly."

Her mother stepped forward, and Harriett could sense the concern in her voice. "You still have time to make your decision."

"It is made. Nothing can change it now." She gave a shaky smile and began pounding out the notes on the sheet music in front of her.

"Very well." Her mother appeared more confused than surprised, shaking her head. "We will resume our preparations. You should tell William. He deserves to know." With that her mother left the room, her yellow skirts brushing past the doorway.

Harriett's hands paused on the keys and she took a deep breath. She had never felt such physical pain in her heart, an ache that threaded down her arms and into her fingers. She played the lively song again and again, hoping it would calm her. It didn't work. Even as the sky outside the window brewed a storm, her heart brewed a darker one.

To distract herself, she spent the afternoon practicing the pianoforte and even stepped outside to draw, despite the growing cold. Rain began to fall, so she went upstairs to her room. At dinner she tried to appear as if nothing was wrong, forcing herself to eat and smile and talk of her upcoming season. After preparing for bed, she crawled under the covers. She couldn't sleep. What could William be thinking of her right now?

She pressed her head into her pillow, anger and confusion flooding her. Her dream of going to London was finally coming true. Then why did she feel terrified—terrified that she would never be happy again? She was terrified that the moment she left Brighton she would be abandoning her happiness, her heart, and her dearest friend.

William had robbed her of her dream, and in the process, he had become her new one.

A dream she would now never have.

Her eyes shot open, and she kicked off her blankets, the heat of her emotions too much to bear. She had a sudden and strange urge to go to the ocean. She needed something bigger than herself, bigger than her own troubles, and something that terrified her more than the things she felt for William Harrison. It was past midnight, but she jumped out of her bed and grabbed her cloak and boots from her wardrobe, careful not to disturb her sleeping parents as she tiptoed down the stairs, out the front door, and into the night air.

Chapter 18

"My poor William. Please do not fret. You will recover your memory eventually, the physician is quite certain of it." His mother sat beside him in the dark library, the place he had taken as his refuge from the turmoil his life had become.

His memory was no longer his greatest concern. His thoughts would not leave Harriett. He wanted to relieve her of the guilt she must have felt. He needed to see her, to assure her all over again that he knew the truth but that it changed nothing. He had poured his heart out to her the day before, but they had been interrupted. All day he had been hoping that she would come. He had tried to give himself the strength to go to her again, but he had remained at home. His mother had insisted upon it, and he had felt too weak to defy her this time.

If Harriett still doubted his devotion, then the only

thing he could do would be to regain his memory. Once she knew that he fully remembered everything, she would have no reason to doubt him. But his brain was still holding up an impenetrable wall around the things he sought to understand.

"We must do all we can to help you retrieve your memories," his mother said, her voice soft and comforting. "You might try bathing in the Brighton waters? I have never experienced the healing qualities myself, but I suspect there is some truth behind it. Is there nothing else you can do that might aid the process?"

He shook his head in frustration. "No, I have tried every—"

He stopped. The Brighton waters. He remembered the painting he had found in his house of the girl by the ocean, the girl he knew to be Harriett. He thought of the emotions it had stirred up inside him. That was the closest he had ever felt to his memories. He had felt them sneaking close to the surface of his mind, almost close enough to touch. He sat up straight with a jolt, an idea setting his heart pounding.

"Mama, I must go. I will return shortly."

She frowned. "It is far too late! You mustn't go."

"I must. I am going to dip in the waters, just as you suggested." He wasn't truly going for a dip, of course, but he had a different plan in mind.

"Not at this hour!" His mother gasped as he rushed out the library door.

If the painting had given him such a closeness to his memories, then what would happen if he visited the exact location of the painting? He had determined that the painting had been created from a small hill near Weston Manor, one that overlooked a particularly smooth section of the beach, where the small pebbles had been weathered down to a finer texture, one closer to that of sand. The painting depicted a dark, stormy sky, much like the one displayed tonight.

With eagerness in his stride, he exited the house and set out for the coastline.

Harriett hadn't expected the water to be so cold. She had gathered the courage to take off her boots and dip her feet in the water that lapped up over the shore. She knew how unwise it was to be outside in the dark alone, but she had been unable to stay within the confines of her house any longer. She hadn't been *this* close to the sea for years, and each time she came near, it filled her with dread and terror. Her chest seized with panic as a wave came close to the shore. She stepped back, watching it crash softly against the sand.

Her pulse returned to normal as she wrapped her cloak more tightly around her. The sand was cold beneath her toes, but not unbearable. She closed her eyes, letting the chilled water and sand calm her body, even as her legs shook beneath her.

Away from the solid walls of her home, the influence of William's mother, and the expectations she had placed over herself, the wind and mist around her began its work untethering her emotions. She had kept them confined, burning like a furnace inside her. Covering it from view had done nothing to smother the flames.

She drew a shuddering breath as she watched the dark sea, rising and falling with the wind. If the wind could command such dangerous waters to rise and fall, what could it do to her weak heart? Could it lead her to defy Mrs. Harrison and make the foolish decision to risk her family's comfort? Could it give her the courage to stay and be with William?

She tightened her grip on her elbows, pulling her arms firmly against her. No. She could not hurt anyone else, and to cancel her trip to London would hurt her family more than anything. She simply needed to be strong.

With her decision made, she turned around. She needed to leave before any of her family woke up and found her missing. As she walked up the bank, she froze. A man stood nearby, shadowed by the darkness. Her heart pounded. She couldn't move. She glanced down at the ground, hoping to find a large rock she could use as a weapon if he came closer. What had she been thinking coming out here so late alone? It seemed she had not gained any wisdom in the years since she had tried to swim in the ocean.

"Who are you?" She tried to keep steady, but she sounded even more frightened than she felt.

"Harriett?" The man's voice threaded goosebumps up her arms.

"William?"

"Yes, it is me. What the devil are you doing out here alone?" He walked closer, and she took an instinctive step backward. Her heart pounded, ached. As he drew closer, she could see him more clearly in the moonlight. His hair fell over his forehead, his eyes shadowed, his mouth serious. He wore a jacket over his white shirt, no cravat tied on his neck. He looked handsome, unjustly so.

"I could ask the same question of you." She crossed her arms tighter, as if it would hide the truth of her emotions. She hoped the darkness would conceal the tears that burned in her eyes. She needed to leave. What if Mrs. Harrison found out that she had seen William? "I simply could not sleep, and thought I would take a walk."

He stared at her, his gaze piercing and firm, as if he were trying to solve her like a puzzle. "My mother advised that I come take a dip in the infamous Brighton waters," he said. "She thought it might heal my mind and give my memories back to me."

Harriett couldn't hide her surprise. Or her terror. "I thought you didn't know how to swim." She would not let him get in that water. The very thought sent her breath speeding up and her palms sweating. "At any rate, the water is far too cold at this time of year."

He smiled softly. "Not to worry, I'm not here to take a dip. You know how I enjoy defying my mother."

A new surge of pain struck her. If only she had the option to defy his mother too. "Then what are you doing here?"

"I thought I might find some of my memories out here. I never thought I would find you." He rubbed his boot over the sand, watching it as he traced circles. "Have you given any further thought to what I said yesterday?"

She nodded, swallowing the grief that choked her. "I am leaving."

He looked up, his eyes filled with hurt and confusion. "What?"

"I have to."

"Why?" He stepped closer, threatening her resolve once again. "Yesterday you said that you cared for me. Were the things I said not enough to convince you?"

"No, William, I—" She shook her head at the ground. "I cannot explain it, but I have to go."

"You do not have to."

"Yes I do!" Her sudden anger seemed to shock him.

His expression fell, his own voice rising with hurt. "Are you still convinced that I am not enough for you? I know I do not have much, but I will always take care of you, Harriett."

She shook her head again, fighting the weakness of her heart. She willed herself to stay strong as she stared up at him. "I cannot stay, William, and I cannot marry you." She again hoped he couldn't see the tears that burned in her eyes, or hear the way her voice shook.

He crossed his arms, casting his eyes upward at the sky, the dim moonlight reflecting off the prominent parts of his face. When his gaze met hers again, it was unrelenting. "If you tell me now that you do not love me, I will leave you alone forever. If what you said to me those years ago was true, then say it again." He took a step closer. "Say you do not love me."

She struggled for words, her tears beginning their fall down her cheeks, dripping from her chin and onto the wet sand. She told herself to lie, to say it, but the wind, the ocean, and William's touch had made her weak, weak enough to pull a whisper from behind the walls of her heart. "I cannot say that."

He groaned and took one step closer, pulling her to him. Before she could take a single breath he was kissing her. One arm slid around her waist, the other held the side of her face. His fingers buried in her hair, and his lips moved firmly over hers, conscious and fervent. Everything she had been holding back from William came pouring into that kiss as she gripped the fabric of his shirt, pulling him impossibly closer. Every bit of hesitation was gone for the briefest moment, every doubt, every fear. Her lungs burned like they did when she had nearly drowned, but kissing William was even more dangerous, even more careless. He whispered her name, and then he kissed her with renewed fervor, the ardent force of his lips enough to awaken her senses. She knew it had to stop. It was cruel and unfair.

She pulled back, pushing against his chest. "William, stop," she said, her voice hoarse as she struggled to catch her breath. His chest rose and fell under her hands, and she felt his heart beating through his shirt. Tears fell fresh down her face, and she shook her head hard. "I have to go to London. I have promised my family. My uncle has invested so much in me. I cannot disappoint them again. When I am gone, I'm certain your memories will return. You will not even miss me."

He stared at her, his jaw clenched. "You are really going?"

She couldn't explain it to him. If his mother found out, she could never forgive herself. "I have no other choice." She kept her lips pressed firmly together, her lips that still tingled from William's kiss. It was all so very unfair. "I have to go."

Before she could cry again, she turned away, picked up her boots, and ran. She didn't stop running until she reached her house, but she didn't go inside. She leaned against the cool stone, hoping it would calm the shaking heat in her limbs, repair the ache in her heart. She had never felt so helpless or so alone. But for her family's sake she would smile as she left for London. She would find joy in her mother's joy, in her uncle's, and would do all she could to find a match that would make them proud. Perhaps there was another man in the world that she could love as much as she loved William. Certainly there was.

She had never told herself a greater lie than that.

Chapter 19

It was hours later when William finally took the short walk back home. He had stayed by the ocean long after Harriett left. There was nothing more he could do to keep her from leaving. She wanted London more than she wanted him it seemed. What more could he have done to convince her? He had been close—so close—to changing her mind, but nothing had worked. His heart felt heavier than it had ever been as he walked through the front door of his family's house just before dawn.

The house was quiet and dim as he made his way across the entry hall. His body felt exhausted, but his mind remained alert, keen to the sense of sorrow that now throbbed through his veins. He turned down the hall that led to his bedchamber, pausing when he saw his mother standing near the doorway. Her hair fell raggedly down the shoulders of her nightdress, and her face was grim.

"William," she said, her voice hushed and firm. "Where have you been?"

He set his jaw, unwilling to discuss his pain and heartache with his mother, who had such a deeply rooted hatred for the woman he loved. He couldn't bear to hear one ill word about Harriett. Although she had hurt him, he knew her dream of going to London was stronger than her love for him. He knew her doubts were unyielding. "That is really none of your concern, mother."

She caught his arm as he passed. "Of course it is! What sort of mother would I be if I allowed you to behave in such a rakish manner? I saw you with Miss Weston out the window, William. I saw everything." Her eyes glinted like steel.

"What gave you the idea to spy on me?"

"I was worried about you, and now I see I have great reason to have been worried." His mother's entire face sparked with anger. "Did you organize this clandestine, scandalous meeting with Miss Weston?"

"No. It was purely coincidental. And you have nothing to worry over mother, I assure you, Miss Weston is going to London. Her decision is final." He pulled his arm from her grasp. He hated the look of pleasure on his mother's face.

"How could a chance encounter at the beach after dark be coincidental? What woman would venture out of her house alone at such an hour?" His mother shook her head with disapproval. "And I never thought you to be such a rake. My own son!"

He turned on her. "I intended to marry her, but she would not have me."

"She must not love you if she is still planning to leave."

William felt another stabbing pain in his heart. She had refused to deny that she loved him. It did not make sense. Her tears had betrayed her own resistance to leaving. Did she truly care more for possessions and titles than for him? He couldn't believe it to be true. "I do not understand why she is leaving." His voice broke. It was just another question that he did not have the answer to.

He wanted to know how he had felt about Harriett before the accident, he wanted to know what the blasted letter from her sister had entailed, and he wanted to know why Harriett was willing to sacrifice her own happiness to go to London. He could see that she no longer wanted to go.

He closed his eyes as he leaned against the wall.

"Oh, William, I do hate to see you in such despair. I will introduce you to Miss Bringhurst and all will be well again. Miss Weston will be away in another town where she cannot hurt you. I will keep you safe from her, just as I always have."

William chose to ignore her words, moving past her and into his room. She didn't protest as he closed the door between them. Something in his mother's voice chilled him, sending tendrils of ice over his spine.

The days passed slowly, and did nothing to soften the prevalent ache in William's heart, nor the frustration he felt at the many questions that still lay unanswered. It had been two weeks since he had seen Harriett at the beach—a fortnight since she had pushed him away forever. He had tried to keep busy studying, and it had helped him remember more and more of his profession.

He had also begun to recall brief passages of time starting at the youngest years of his childhood and working closer to the present. The memories were still clouded over with uncertainty, as if they did not fully belong to him. But he knew he was growing closer to claiming them all. He tried his best to rid his thoughts of Harriett, but she was the one thing he seemed incapable of forgetting.

William found Maria at the breakfast bar one morning. She, like everyone else, seemed to have been avoiding him. She met his gaze with a warm smile, but it quickly fell as her large eyes took in his expression. "What is the matter, William?"

He had discovered that he was not adept at hiding his emotions. He had been asked what the matter was far too many times of late. It was fortunate that he had found Maria alone, for he was not afraid to confide in her. She was the most trustworthy person in his family, and his mother was quickly becoming the least. His suspicion toward her had grown along with his awareness of his past. She had seemed all too pleased to have Harriett on her way out of his life forever.

"I am very confused over a great number of things," he said. "I wondered if you might help me understand them." As he stared down at the food on the sidebar, he had no interest in any of it, despite the pangs of hunger in his stomach.

"That is to be expected, of course, considering your current condition." Maria spoke innocently, without the false hope that others tried to convey. "I would love to help you."

"I knew I could trust you."

She smiled. "I am glad to hear you have such great faith in me." She placed a piece of bread on her plate and began spreading orange preserves over the top.

"I suspect you know how I feel about Harriett Weston."

Maria's eyes widened in surprise. Her hands stalled. "Have you finally come to accept your feelings? I have always known you secretly loved her. I always suspected she loved you as well. She often asked about you, inquiring after your health and such."

He sighed. "Do you believe she would ever choose to marry for advantage over love? She still intends to go to London for a season."

"Well, have you declared your feelings to her?"

"Yes."

Maria's brow creased. "Did she refuse you?"

"She did. Mother was quite pleased."

Biting her lower lip, Maria turned her attention back to the food on her plate, making one last selection of a slice of ham before turning toward him. "Yes, I can imagine she was quite pleased indeed."

He picked up a tone of secrecy in Maria's voice, one that triggered a warning in his mind. "You know Mother better than I do in my current state. What lengths do you suppose Mother might have taken to ensure that I did not marry Harriett?"

Maria shifted uncomfortably, her round cheeks growing pink. He saw in her eyes—burning with remorse—a secret. "She would go to great lengths, I'm afraid." Maria glanced behind her at the door before motioning for William to join her at the table. "She made me promise not to tell you. I only heard about it yesterday."

William's heart seized in anticipation.

"I felt terrible about keeping it a secret from you." Her

eyes filled with tears. "But you know how demanding Mama can be."

He touched her arm softly as she sniffed, wiping her nose. "You must tell me, Maria. Please. I will ensure Mother does nothing to hurt you."

"No, no, she would never hurt me or any of her children." Maria laughed softly before her expression grew serious. "But she would certainly hurt Miss Weston and her family if it means protecting her child from a threat that only she can see."

"Harriett."

Maria nodded. "Mama called on Harriett a fortnight ago. She told her that our family would not invest in the Weston's horses and land, leaving them at the risk of further financial insecurity, if Harriett were ever to see you again."

It felt as though a rock had settled in William's stomach. He sat back in his chair as the realization sunk in. Anger pulsed inside him. "Thank you for telling me."

She gave a shaky smile. "You do not deserve to be unhappy, especially at the hands of your own mother."

"Nor do you. I will ensure she does nothing to punish you."

Maria thanked him, and he gave her hand a squeeze before standing from his place at the table. William knew his mother spent her mornings in the library. The fierce anger that had sprung inside him quickly transformed to feelings of betrayal as he made his way down the hall. As he had expected, his mother sat in a chair by the fireplace, a book open on her lap.

She glanced up as he entered. "Ah, William, how are you this morning? I trust you slept well."

"I know what you did," he said.

His mother stilled, staring at him for a long moment

before turning her gaze back down to her book. "I do not know what on earth you mean."

He took one step into the room. "You threatened to retract your purchases of Mr. Weston's horses and property in order to ensure Harriett never saw me again. You threatened her."

She seemed intent to deny it, her features springing into defensiveness, but after a few seconds they relaxed. "Yes, I did. I did it for you. At the moment you are not capable of making your own rational decisions. As your mother, I must do all I can to protect you in your current state of ignorance."

"It is not I who is ignorant, mother, it is you."

She gasped, her eyes narrowing. "I have every memory of your joyful days as a child, playing with your friends. I have every memory of the lighthearted boy you were. I still recall the day you came home, soaked to the bone, after having saved Miss Weston's life, and nearly drowning. I saw that you no longer wished to play with your friends, that you were embarrassed and hurt and changed by something that despicable girl said to you. Not only did she nearly take your life, but she took my joyful little boy from me." She choked on a breath. "I could not let her take you from me again."

The vehemence behind her words shocked him, and he walked closer to where she sat in her chair. She appeared suddenly frailer, more broken and fragile. Drawing a heavy breath, she gripped the sides of her chair. "And then, on your trip with your father, her meddlesome sister wrote you a letter that drew you back to Brighton in a most dangerous fashion, causing you to fall off your horse and nearly die again."

William stopped. He had nearly forgotten about the

letter that he and Maria had been so curious about. "The letter? How do you know about the letter?"

Her gaze lifted to his, heavy with the first hint of regret he could remember seeing on her face. She stood in a rustle of heavy fabric, crossing the room to the writing desk. From behind the cover of a book, she withdrew a folded piece of parchment. "I found this in your jacket when I came to see you while you were still unconscious." Her voice was rasped as she extended it to him. "I could only presume that this letter was what compelled you to end your trip early and make your rampage through the woods toward the Weston home." She shook her head. "I suppose you always did love that despicable girl." She glanced at the ground in a look that William could only view as shameful. "I should not have kept it from you. It would have brought you a great deal of clarity, but I could not fathom taking any part in fostering a union between you and Miss Weston. But it seems there was nothing I could do to stop you from pursuing that young lady once you set your mind to it."

William took the letter slowly from her shaking hand. He studied her firm, lined face, surprised to see it so ashamed. "You did not call her despicable that time," he said.

A faint smile touched his mother's lips, one so subtle he thought he had imagined it. "No, it seems I did not." Her eyes still downcast, she flicked her wrist in his direction. "Now read it before I change my mind and cast it into the fire."

He unfolded the worn letter, his pulse bounding as he found the first line. The handwriting blurred in front of his eyes. It was familiar, each stroke cutting through the cloudiness of his mind like a dagger.

To Mr. William Harrison

I know this letter is of a most unconventional manner, but I could not remain silent on a certain subject any longer. I know that you and my sister Harriett were once very dear friends. I do not know fully what happened between you, for Harriett will not speak of it no matter how dearly I press her, but I do have reason to believe that my sister still cares for you deeply. She misses you. I can see it in her eyes at every event in which you are in attendance. I see the same reactions in you, and while I cannot understand what has been keeping the two of you apart all these years, I know without a doubt that whatever it is, it can be overcome by love. Love can overcome hatred, doubt, and any measure of resentment, of that I am most certain.

Our Uncle Cornelius is soon to surprise Harriett with a season in London, and my family has the highest hopes of her marriage there. I have reason to believe that they would be quite pleased still if you managed to woo Harriett instead. They, just as much as I, have no greater wish than to see her truly happy. Now, this entire letter may be awfully presumptuous of me, and in such a case, please disregard these words. If, however, you feel as I suspect, then you must act. Be brave, William, just as you taught us to be brave in the face of wicked pirates and sea monsters during those childhood days on the beach.

Sincerely,

Lady Coventry

He had not expected it all to come at once, but, like a bolt of lighting, sudden clarity flooded his mind. He remembered the day he first read the letter. He remembered the feeling of hope, sprouting up from a place it had been long buried. He recalled every event in which he had seen Harriett Weston, from the day he returned from university until the day he left for his hunting trip. He felt keenly the fear he had felt in his heart to approach her, the fear of being rejected and turned away again each time he saw her. Even Harriett's words to him on the beach when they were children came flooding back to his recollection.

He remembered his mother after that, fiercely protective, keeping him inside during every storm, keeping a close watch on him near the water's edge. Keeping him far away from Harriett Weston.

His entire life returned to his mind as if he had just opened his eyes to a new world. His perception of his surroundings changed, the familiarity of it shocking. His mother's face became endearing, a face he had relied on for so many years, the shelves of books around him changed, now connected with memories of tutoring sessions from his father, of Percival sitting at the table poring over his favorite books. Amid it all, one thing had not changed. He still loved Harriett. He loved her even more than he had before, and he knew, without a doubt, that he had to stop her from leaving him.

His mother's mouth had become a firm line, her brows drawn together. "You look rather pale. Please sit down."

He laughed, the sound bursting out with strange independence. He held his head between his hands as he paced closer to his mother. "I remember everything."

"Everything? Your memories have returned?" Tears immediately sprung to her eyes. "Oh, my sweet William, I knew it would happen eventually."

"You have Miss Harriett Weston to thank for it."

Her smile faltered a bit at that statement, but he leaned forward and kissed her cheek. Despite all she had done to hurt him, she was still his mother. He hardened his gaze to emphasize his words. "Promise me you will not hurt Harriett or her family, and you will not punish Maria for telling me what you did."

His mother's tears fell over her cheeks, catching in the wrinkles below her eyes. She sobbed, casting her eyes heavenward. "Harriett Weston has saved you! She has helped recover your memories, how could I hate her now?" She tossed her hands in the air. "Go after her, William, if you must, but please do not ride with such carelessness this time."

William backed away, utterly confused by his mother's behavior, but hopeful at her new demand. *Go after her.* He pushed past the library doors, energy pulsing through his body. It was mid December, and the season wasn't set to begin until January. He could still stop her if she knew that her family was safe from his mother's schemes.

Chapter 20

William ran over the frosted back lawn to the stables, mounted his horse, and then entering the trees. As he rode along the path, he recalled every moment of his ride the day he returned to Brighton, the wind whipping past his skin, his pulse racing with fear and determination… but he couldn't remember the fall. As his horse leapt carefully through the clearing with the fallen tree, he thanked his good fortune that Harriett had been there that day.

When he reached the Weston's property, he dismounted and tethered his horse to a nearby tree. His breath expelled fog into the air in front of him, the frostbitten grass crunching under his boots as he walked closer to the house.

On the drive, he noticed a fine carriage coming to

a halt. As he came closer, he recognized the man exiting to be Lord Coventry, the former Lord Ramsbury. With his dark blonde hair, fashionable attire, and broad smile, he was unmistakable. He reached into the carriage. A shriek and a laugh followed as he lifted his wife, Grace, from the step, spinning her above the ground before setting her down. She swatted at his arm as he laughed.

He recognized Grace clearly. He had never thought she would pursue a man like Lord Ramsbury. He did not know the man's character well, but he knew enough to assume he was a rake. But William had learned that people were often not what they seemed, and all people were capable of change.

At William's approach, Grace glanced around her husband, catching William's gaze. He waved with a smile. He had not spoken to her at length in years, but had always offered a polite greeting when he saw her.

"Mr. William Harrison, is that you?" Grace smiled, her brown eyes dancing as he stopped beside them. Her smile took on a mischievous twist as she shared a glance with her husband. She returned her attention to William. "What has brought you here? We just returned last night from Berwick and thought to come visit my family."

"Is your sister home?"

Grace looked as if she were on the brink of bursting with excitement. "Did you finally receive my letter? I sent it months ago. I cannot imagine why it took so long to arrive."

He nodded, not feeling it necessary to explain that he *had* received it months ago, but had simply forgotten all about it.

"I believe Harriett is inside." She waved the hand that

was not holding her husband's, ushering William toward the front doors. "She will be so happy to see you, I am certain."

William hoped she was right. What if Harriett still insisted on leaving because she truly cared about London and finding a wealthy match more than she cared about him? He shunned the thought, taking a deep breath of fortitude as Lord Coventry knocked on the door.

The butler let them all in, offering Grace a warm smile of welcome. William had been well acquainted with the Weston's butler over the last several months as he had called upon Harriett so many times. When the butler's eyes caught on him, his smile fell.

"Mr. Harrison has come to see Harriett," Grace told him, her voice slightly hushed, as if she were telling a rapturous secret. William caught the deep chuckle from Lord Coventry as he listened. Grace turned toward William. "Would you like a private audience with her? I'm certain that could be arranged quite easily."

William couldn't help but smile. "If it is no trouble."

"No trouble at all," she said.

The butler cleared his throat, and for a moment William thought he would claim Harriett to be ill again. Because of his mother, Harriett still thought she had to stay away from him to protect her family. He needed to see her and explain that there was no longer anything that could prevent them from being together. The butler addressed Grace. "Your sister and mother departed for London last week, I'm afraid. They meant to inform you, but the letter would not have reached you in your travels home."

William's heart sank. He stepped forward. "The season does not begin until the new year."

"Yes, but it is to my understanding that Miss Weston

was quite eager to depart, and her mother thought it wise to ensure their town house was properly decorated for any visitors they might receive upon the start of the season."

Grace exchanged a look of pure deflation with her husband before turning her gaze back to William. "I thought she would be here."

William swallowed the disappointment that had risen in his throat, the sorrow that had begun to throb against his heart. "As did I."

A loud, boisterous voice came from within the house, and the man William knew to be Harriett's uncle, The Baron of Hove, came forward. "Is that my Grace?"

Her smile returned, but it was half-hearted as she squeezed her uncle's hands in greeting. "Uncle Cornelius, I am so happy to see you."

"I trust your travels were quite comfortable?"

"Indeed." She glanced over her shoulder at William, and the baron's sharp blue eyes found his.

"Ah, Mr. Harrison! How do you do?"

He felt no need to tell the truth in that moment. "I am quite well, and you?"

"Quite well, indeed. My niece has just departed for London, and I miss her dearly, but I am glad to have Grace back in town."

William nodded, careful to hide his dejection at the confirmation that Harriett was indeed in London. There was nothing William could do now but wait for her to return, and hope that she did not find a different man to marry. The very idea set his heart reeling.

"Has Miss Weston been long departed?" William asked.

"Oh, she made her departure a week ago at least."

Grace's expression had grown increasingly troubled. "It

is not too late! You might go to London and stop her. She loves you William, I know she does."

William couldn't believe that Grace would suggest he do such a thing in the presence of her uncle, who had funded the entire season. He eyed the baron, whose gaze darted between Grace and William with intense curiosity. After a long moment of silence, he gasped. "I knew it was true!" A slow smile crept onto his lips, lifting the gray whiskers on his cheeks. "Her mother came to tell me that she wished to stay in Brighton and marry you, Mr. Harrison, but then something changed her mind. I found the entire situation to be quite odd. Do you love her too?"

William nodded. "Very much."

"Ah!" The baron clapped his hands together. "I always knew it! That must have been the reason her enthusiasm seemed to decrease quite considerably about her season." He tapped his chin. "You must go to London at once! I daresay there will be plenty of gentlemen seeking her attention this evening, but only one whose attention she will happily receive." He winked.

William stood in shock. "Are you certain?"

Lord Hove swished his hand through the air. "No investment is worth sacrificing my niece's happiness. If I find out she went to London just to please me, I will be fit to be tied." He paused. "I have always been quite fond of your sister Maria. She is quite an amiable young lady, and handsome as well. I daresay with a few alterations Harriett's numerous gowns will fit her quite nicely, and the lease on the townhouse has already been paid. Do you suppose she and your mother might like to spend the season in London in Harriett's place? Considering she accepts your proposal and returns to Brighton, of course."

William couldn't believe the baron's generosity and understanding. He struggled for words. If the baron knew that his mother had been responsible for keeping William and Harriett apart, would he still insist on sending Maria to London? Maria had been dreaming of London for as long as William could remember—and that was now much longer than it had previously been.

"I cannot thank you enough for you generosity," William said. "Perhaps with a different chaperone than my mother, Maria would have a wonderful time."

The baron didn't question it. "We can certainly arrange something to Maria's satisfaction."

"Thank you," William repeated.

Lord Hove grinned. "It is no problem at all. I was in love once, Mr. Harrison. I know how it feels to lose the one you love, and I would never wish it upon anyone."

"Are you certain it is not too great a sacrifice?" William could hardly believe the man's kindness.

"What is love if it isn't worth every sacrifice?" Lord Hove smiled.

Grace squealed with delight, and Lord Coventry laughed.

"Take our coach," Lord Coventry said. "It is already prepared and waiting on the drive. I will bring your horse into the stables while you are away."

Lord Hove excused himself, hurrying from the room to fetch a paper and pencil with which to give William the address of the townhouse Harriett was staying in on St. James's square.

After Lord Hove returned, William took off across the grass, Lord and Lady Coventry cheering as he went. After handing the address to the coachman, he set off for London.

Chapter 21

Sitting by the window of her new London residence, Harriett picked up the letter her father had forwarded to her from Grace. It had arrived shortly after she left for London, and had been delivered just minutes before.

Dearest Harriett,

I suspect you are lying to me. How can you imply that William has not shown any interest in you? I did not wish to tell you this, because I knew you would be very angry with me, but please know that I did it for your own good.

I doubted that you would actually pursue William as you promised in our wager. I knew how difficult it would be for you, and I knew you were quite afraid. As I puzzled over what I might do to help, I thought that I had no other choice but to push William in the right direction. I knew that even with the smallest spark of hope he would come and steal your heart. I can picture you reading this with one of your scowls, and perhaps you are cursing my name to the wind, but if you are indeed lying to me about your feelings for William, then I must conclude that you are also lying to yourself.

Uncle Cornelius told me of his plans to surprise you with a season even before I took my trip to the north. Of course I am happy for you, but I wanted to ensure you had a chance to see William again before you left and found a less worthy man to marry. So, allow me to tell you what I did to push William in the right direction.

I wrote him a letter. I sent it to Maria, who was instructed to send it to William at his hunting lodge. I will not 'bore you with the details' but just know that the letter was very clear on the point that William had a very limited time to win your affection, although I suspected he still had it. That is the point of my confusion. I cannot believe that William wouldn't have made a greater effort to win you over. I suppose when I return to Brighton, I may set to work discovering the truth behind all this mystery.

With love,

Grace

Harriett set the letter down in her lap, her heart pounding with the sorrow she had been hiding. So William had loved her all along, even before his accident. He had come back from his trip early for her. He had been on his way to see her when he was thrown from his horse in the woods. The realization set her hands shaking. She wondered if his memories had returned yet. She wondered if she would ever see him again.

The first week in London had passed like a storm, beautiful and breathtaking. But the moment it had begun, Harriett wished it would end.

Standing from her place by the dim light of the window, she smoothed the skirts of her ball gown. She and her mother were attending a public assembly, one that was set to begin in a few short minutes. She dreaded it.

"Come, we mustn't be late," her mother walked into the room, straightening her gloves and the feathers in her satin turban.

Harriett stood, following her mother out to the street where their coach awaited them. After stepping inside, she fixed her gaze out the window.

Although the season had yet to officially begin, many eligible gentlemen and young ladies had already arrived, and were planning on attending the ball that evening. Harriett wore her favorite dress that had been made for the season, a pale blue gown with a sheer ivory over-sleeve that reached her wrists. The ribbon at her waist matched the one she had debated over with her mother, when William had seen them in town.

The very thought of his name pierced her with grief. She pushed away the new memories of him—of his arms around her, his kiss, the weight she had seen in his eyes when she broke his heart a second time. The worst of it was that she could not explain why she had left him. That haunted her more than anything else.

For her mother's sake, she pretended to be enjoying London, but in truth, it was not all she had dreamed it would be. It was crowded and stiff, with buildings at every turn. The gardens were lovely, but there was no ocean to be seen. She didn't think she would ever miss the sea so much. But she had come to associate it with the last time she had seen William, so how could she not miss it when she missed him so much?

A few minutes later, she and her mother entered the ballroom. Harriett blinked as she surveyed the glittering candles, the beautiful dresses, and the fine architecture of the building. The entire room felt stifling, hot, and musty. Her mother squeezed her elbow softly. "There are already many eyes on you, my dear."

Harriett did not want many eyes on her, but as she surveyed the room again, she found that her mother was right. Several gentleman had glanced in her direction, letting their gazes linger on her for longer than her mother had taught her was appropriate. She accidentally met the lingering gaze of one tall blond gentleman. She combed her mind for the lesson her mother had given her about deflecting the attention of an undesirable man. Despite her every instinct to look down at the ground, she quickly turned to her mother, remembering that it was best to begin a conversation with someone nearby after cutting off eye contact.

She exhaled through her nostrils. The anxiety she was experiencing at being in the ballroom felt as if it might crush her. How could she endure months of this when her heart was back in Brighton? She could never fall in love with any of these men. They were not William.

"What are you doing?" her mother hissed through her teeth.

"What do you mean?"

"That is the Viscount of Helston."

Harriett couldn't quite comprehend how her mother

had known exactly which gentleman Harriett had glanced away from. "Oh. I did not know."

"If he looks at you again you must remember to hold his gaze for several seconds, offer a small smile like the one we practiced, and then glance bashfully at the ground. Remember, you mustn't stare for too long, and you must never approach him. He will come to you."

Harriett nodded solemnly, earning a smile from her mother.

"Try again."

"Again?"

"Glance at him as we pass, and hold his gaze longer this time. I suspect he will attempt to be introduced to you and claim at least one dance, perhaps two." Her mother took her arm, guiding her through the crowd. Harriett's stomach twisted with dread as they came closer to the viscount and his friends, where they stood gathered in a circle near the master of ceremonies.

She kept her gaze firmly on the ground until they were in close proximity, then lifted her gaze. She misjudged his location, however, her eyes landing instead on a man that stood near the entrance. Her heart seized when she recognized the warm green eyes and dark auburn hair of William. Her breath caught. It couldn't be him. Surely she was imagining it. Her heart hammered so hard it hurt, and she stopped like a rebellious horse as her mother tried to pull her along.

"Harriett," her mother whispered. "You have been staring for much too long."

She hardly heard her. William—she was now certain it was him—met her gaze from across the room. *What was he doing here?* She commanded her feet to remain planted, but they betrayed her, pushing her away from her mother's side, moving her closer to William. He met her halfway, his eyes warm and smiling as he looked down at her.

"William," Harriett said in a hushed voice. "What are you doing in London?" She tried to memorize every detail of his face. His eyes, clear and green, the line of his nose, the creases at the corners of his eyes, and the graceful upturn of the corners of his mouth as he smiled down at her. What reason could he have to be smiling? Her own heart felt torn to pieces at his arrival, knowing that she would have to send him away all over again. "You should not be here."

"No, I believe I should." His voice was deep, soft, and demanded attention. "Your maid informed me that I had just missed you when I stopped at your London address. She was kind enough to give me the location of the ball."

"I told you that I could never see you again."

"I know what my mother did."

She blinked up at him. "You do?"

"Maria told me everything."

The realization sunk in slowly, and hope grew like a barren rose blossoming inside her. "Have you found a way to stop her?"

"I have." William smiled softly. "In fact, I think she may be growing to like you."

Harriett shook her head hard, her shock still searing over her skin. William was *here*? "That cannot be possible. What has changed her mind?"

"Your sister sent me a letter before I returned to Brighton."

Harriett could hardly breathe amid the turmoil inside her. She nodded, unable to speak.

"I remember everything, Harriett," he said. "The moment I read the letter I remembered. I remember the day at the ocean that you told me about, and I remember how deeply it hurt me, but I also remember how little it affected how much I cared for you. It made me afraid, that is all, but I'm not afraid anymore. My mother had been hiding the letter, and she now believes you to be the reason my memories returned."

Harriett laughed, a breathless sound. Relief stronger than anything she had ever felt flooded her.

He took a step closer, his voice lowering. "She finally believes how madly in love with you I am."

Many nearby eyes had shifted in their direction, likely planning all the gossip they could about the close proximity in which William stood to Harriett, and about the way he stared down at her with such a sizeable measure of raw adoration.

William looked as if he wanted to say more, but he seemed to notice the attention too. He eyed the door that led to the nearby terrace, empty because of the cold. "Blast it," he muttered, taking Harriett by the arm and guiding her quickly toward the door. They weaved through the guests in the ballroom, and he pulled her outside into the cold.

The moment they were beyond the door, he took her hands tightly in his. His touch sent a stream of warmth through her arms, and the look in his eyes was enough to match it. He pulled her to him, pressing his lips firmly to hers before they could be seen. He wrapped his arms around her waist, his hands sliding over her back, then cupping her face, holding her as if she were the most precious thing in the world. She kissed him like she wished she could have at the beach that night she left his side, as if she were allowed to have him for the rest of her life. And now she knew she could.

His kiss grew gentle, careful, sending hope and peace and love spiraling through her heart. She wished he would never stop. He pulled back, pressing his forehead against hers. She clung to his jacket, her eyes closed as he brushed another tantalizing kiss, then another across her lips.

"I love you, William," she whispered, opening her eyes to meet his. "I cannot believe you are here."

His face split into a smile. "Does that mean you'll marry me?"

She laughed, unable to stop the tears that spilled over her eyes, tears of unconquerable joy, something she had feared she could never feel again. Her laugh bubbled out again. "I always did believe I would find my husband in London."

He tipped his head back with a hearty laugh. "Yet you once said you doubted I could find a wife in London."

"I only said that because I was quite jealous at the thought. I didn't know all along that it was me."

"Oh, Harriett." He wiped a tear from the side of her face, his smile wide and bright and full of hope. "It was always you."

Find the complete series on Amazon

Brides of Brighton
A CONVENIENT ENGAGEMENT
MARRYING MISS MILTON
ROMANCING LORD RAMSBURY
MISS WESTON'S WAGER
AN UNEXPECTED BRIDE

About the Author

Ashtyn Newbold grew up with a love of stories. When she discovered chick flicks and Jane Austen books in high school, she learned she was a sucker for romantic ones. When not indulging in sweet romantic comedies and regency period novels (and cookies), she writes romantic stories of her own across several genres. Ashtyn also enjoys baking, singing, sewing, and anything that involves creativity and imagination.

www.ashtynnewbold.com

Printed in Great Britain
by Amazon